BEARS OF BLACKROCK

BOOKS ONE - FOUR

LIA DAVIS

AFTER GLOWS PUBLISHING

Bears of Blackrock series

© Copyright 2015-2018 Lia Davis

Published by Davis Raynes Publishing Group, LLC

dba After Glows Publishing

PO Box 224

Middleburg, FL 32050

AfterGlowsPublishing.com

Cover by Lia Davis at Glowing Moon Designs

Formatting by Lia Davis at Glowing Moon Designs

All rights reserved under the International and Pan-American Copyright Conventions. No part of this book may be reproduced or transmitted in any form or by any means, electronic or mechanical, including photocopying, recording, or by any information storage and retrieval system, without permission in writing from the publisher.

This is a work of fiction. Names, places, characters and incidents are either the product of the author's imagination or are used fictitiously, and any resemblance to any actual persons, living or dead, organizations, events or locales is entirely coincidental.

Warning: the unauthorized reproduction or distribution of this copyrighted work is illegal. Criminal copyright infringement, including infringement without monetary gain, is investigated by the FBI and is punishable by up to 5 years in prison and a fine of $250,000.

AfterGlowsPublishing.com

To the love of my life, my rock, and my soul mate

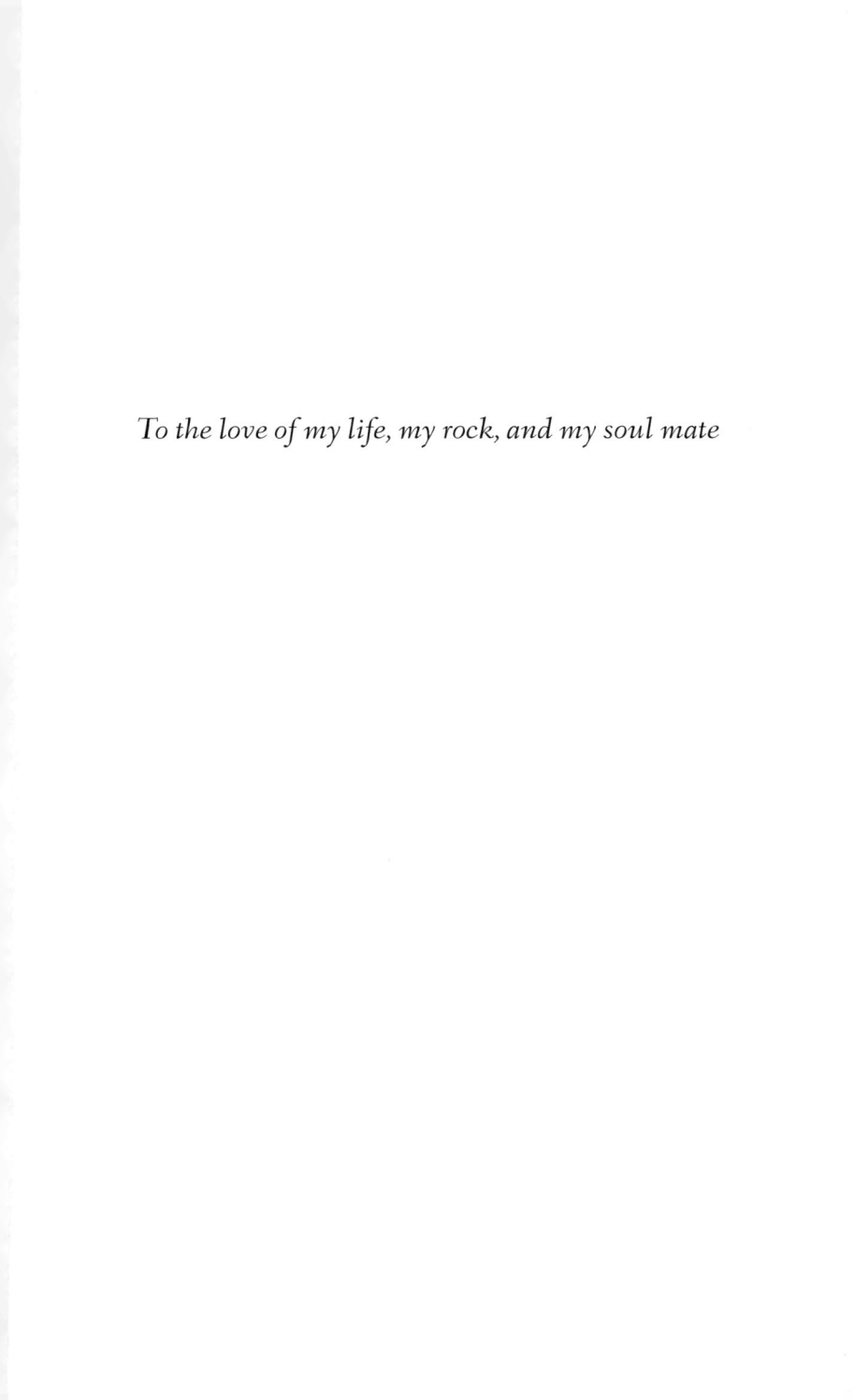

BEAR ESSENTIALS

BEARS OF BLACKROCK, BOOK ONE

Bear Essentials

Fresh from an ugly breakup that trampled her spirit, Nichole just wants to hide away. Unfortunately, her BFF has other plans. Nichole gets dragged to a girls' night out at new club called The Claw, where she meets the intense and gorgeous Trey Black. With eyes that burn and a body built for sin, any woman would sit up and take notice. But why bother? Men like him didn't date women like her.

Trey considers it a good day if he can just stay out of trouble. As the youngest son of the bear Alpha, he's a master at getting his way. When he meets the curvy, raven-haired goddess, Nichole, he realizes exactly what he wants and knows that she's worth any amount of trouble. All he has to do is seduce all of her insecurities away and claim her as his bonded mate.

1

The loud rumble of male laughter erupted from the table next to the entrance of Beary Sweets—a bakery and café located in downtown Blue Ridge, Georgia. Nichole glanced up from her tablet to see three large, gorgeous men filling a booth close to the door. She'd seen them in the café before, but this time was different. They were louder and kept throwing glances at her.

Nichole was tempted to go to the bathroom to check to see if she'd grown another head. But whatever. So what if she had two heads. It'd just be one more thing for men to complain about.

From what she could tell, the men in the booth were brothers. Each had black hair, sky blue eyes, and big, hard bodies. Narrowing her gaze, she noted the two facing her were teasing the one with his back to her. *Not my problem.* She returned her focus to her tablet and her job search.

New rule. Never work with or for the boyfriend. It never ends well.

A sense of hopelessness washed over her as she submitted her resume along with another online application. It was no use. Every company wanted a college degree. Nichole didn't have the drive to return to school. She hadn't needed to.

That had all changed recently, thanks to her insensitive jerk of an ex-boyfriend.

Releasing a sigh, she shut off the tablet, picked up her hazelnut mocha latte and stared out the window. People bustled by the glass, enjoying the warm spring temperatures. Kids skipped beside their parents while holding their hands.

Nichole's chest tightened. God, she longed to be a mother. At age thirty-two, she felt she was losing time. Sure, nowadays women had kids in their forties, but Nichole wanted them now, while she was still young. Not that forty was old.

Silly dreams. All of them shattered, bringing her right back to the reality of her life. The crazy, curvy cat lady. Yep, that was her.

She could always have in vitro fertilization, but that didn't seem to be the right thing for her. No, she held out hope that Mr. Right would walk into her life at any moment.

The table of guys fell silent, still glancing at her. Then the one with his back to her stood. When he turned, his vivid blue eyes bored into her. Heat spread through her like a blast of hot air. He walked...no, he prowled toward her, his large shoulders rolling as he moved. A predator on the hunt.

Her heart hammered when he sat in the seat across from her and leaned over the table. When he spoke, his words came out as a husky, growl-like whisper. "Have dinner with me."

Blinking, she tamped down the urge to touch him. What the hell was wrong with her? "I'm sorry, I don't have dinner with strangers."

The corners of his full mouth lifted. "Forgive me." He offered her his hand. "I'm Trey Black."

She flicked her gaze to the other two men at the front table. They stared at her and the handsome stranger as if eagerly waiting for Trey to score. Not today. All the fire inside her dissolved into a cool mist. She tucked her tablet into her tote and stood. "I'm not interested in middle school games. If you'd like, I can just give you my panties and save you the trouble. That way, you won't look like a total loser in front of your friends."

When she turned, he gripped her wrist. Electrified prickles raced up her arm, awakening the flame once again. "I don't play games. I like you."

She almost laughed. "You could have any woman you want. A perfect model-type. So forgive me if I don't believe you."

Snatching her wrist free from his grasp, she fled past his friends and out the door. Tears stung her eyes as she fumbled with her keys. Men were all the same. They said pretty words to get what they wanted, then tossed her aside like old shoes.

Never again. She'd die an old maid before giving her heart to another again.

∽

TREY STOOD to follow the female out the door, but Tiffany, his sister and owner of Beary Sweets, stepped in his way. "Move, Tif."

"No." She pointed out the door. "She just got her heart ripped out a few months ago by an asshat."

He focused on his sister. She'd gone into mama bear mode. "You know her?"

"I'm friends with her bestie, Connie. We've all gone out a few times." Tiffany folded her arms and glared at Trey, watching his lips set in a thin line. "You need to be gentle with her. Show her you like all of her, including her curves."

Anger brewed in his blood. "What happened?"

She shook her head. "All I'm saying is that those words you spoke, she's heard them before. Then her heart got ripped out when the jerk who said them didn't defend her after his friends were rude about her weight."

Trey fisted his hands and growled low. "What's her name?"

"Nichole."

He smiled as he tossed the name around inside his head. "Where can I find her?"

Tiffany sighed. "Males. We're going to The Claw tonight."

His sister walked off, ending the conversation. Fine by him. He had all the info he needed for the moment. Nichole was his, and he'd never backed down from getting what he wanted before. He wasn't about to start now.

Nichole was going to know what it was like to be loved and pampered by a bear.

2

"You're not ready."

Lifting her gaze from the book she was pretending to read, Nichole considered her friend's words for a few moments before shaking her head. "I've changed my mind. I have work to do."

Connie scowled at her with her hands on her hips. "Liar." Grabbing the book and placing it on the coffee table, the other woman tugged Nichole to a stand. "You're going, and you're going to have a blast."

With a huff, Nichole followed her best friend down the hall. She wanted to hide for a little while longer, not wanting another repeat of that morning at the café. Besides, it didn't take her long to connect the dots. Trey Black was Tiffany's brother.

The chances he'd show up at The Claw were too high for Nichole to risk.

Once inside her bedroom, she sat on the edge of the bed and watched Connie drag an armful of items from her closet. "Who's all going to be there besides Tiffany?"

"Kaylee. She works with Tiffany at Beary Sweets." Connie dropped the clothes onto the bed and grinned. "I think you should wear red. It goes great with your dark hair."

Nichol frowned at the pile. She really didn't want to get out of her comfy sweats and ratty t-shirt. It was fine by her if she never left the house again. However, Connie wouldn't rest until she succeeded in dragging Nichole out.

Connie picked up a cranberry-colored top and handed it to her. "This looks amazing on you."

"Look, Connie, I don't think..."

"No, no. You are going. You are getting out of this house and living again. Don't make me drag you out by your hair." She propped her hands on her hips and glared.

"Nothing looks good on me."

"That's the scum-bastard ex talking right there." Connie stepped in front of her and cupped her chin. "Hon, you are beautiful, every curvy inch of you."

Smiling, Nichole sagged and rested her forehead against Connie's middle. Being a size eighteen had never really bothered her much. Okay, it did, but hearing her ex's friends laugh about her weight and having the jerk not defend her had hurt. They'd dated for a year, and not once had the asshole complained about her size.

She glanced down at the top Connie had given her. "This doesn't fit."

"Yes, it does. Put it on."

Giving up on trying to talk her way out of going, Nichole removed her too-comfortable old tee and put the form-fitting knit top on. Connie pulled her to a stand and dragged her to the full-length closet mirror. "Oh, wait." Connie darted inside the closet and came out with a black lacy scarf. After tying it around Nichole's neck and making a few small tweaks, Connie stepped back and smiled. "Your black jeggings will look perfect with that."

Nichole was about to tell her friend it was no use, but when she caught a glimpse of herself in the mirror, her breath hitched. She'd never worn the top before because she had a green one similar to it that Lee, the ex-bastard, said he didn't like. The woman in the reflection was beautiful. The top hugged her curves to mid-thigh, and the scarf added that something extra that Nichole was sure there was a name for. But she was no fashion expert.

"It looks amazing!"

"I know!" Connie clapped once before she grabbed the black, slim-fit jeans from the bed and tossed them to her, then rushed to the closet. "I think your black heels will look great."

"No. Get the flats."

"Oh!" Connie came out holding a pair of dark red flats Nichole had bought on one of her depressed shopping trips. "You've been hiding shoes from me," her friend teased.

"I bought those the day I told Lee to fuck off."

"They're perfect for that outfit. New shoes for new beginnings."

Nichole wasn't so sure she wanted a new beginning. Not yet. Why couldn't she just veg on the couch for another decade or something?

Because she wasn't the type to give up. Especially because of something that shallow, sorry excuse of a man had done. Reaching out, she took the shoes from her best friend and slipped them on her feet. "New beginnings. Right after we tame my hair."

Connie laughed and hugged her. "I knew you'd be back." Releasing her, Connie stepped back and studied her hair. "Sit. I know the perfect style to try."

Glancing at her reflection, Nichole smiled and smoothed the sweater down over her hips. Sure, she wasn't a perfect size six, but she wasn't ugly. Who needed shallow, ego-maniacal men who wanted a doll on their arm anyway?

Not this girl.

≈

Trey settled into a corner booth and scanned the growing crowd at The Claw—a nightclub owned by Donovan, the bear Elder of his Pack, Blackrock. Only a handful of tables were empty. That wouldn't last, not on a Friday night. A soft female laugh drifted over the low chatter, drawing his attention to his sister, Tiffany, as she and her friend from the café walked toward him.

Tiffany wore her straight, black hair loose to cascade over her shoulders. She had the signature blue eyes his family was known for and their mother's five-foot-four height and curves. His lips twitched as she bounced to a stop in front of him.

"Hi, Trey. You know Kaylee." Tiffany gestured to her friend.

With a short nod, Trey motioned for them to have a seat. "Yes, we've met at Beary Sweets."

Kaylee dipped her head with a shy smile and slid into the seat next to Tiffany. "Hi."

"Hi." The blonde female was pretty with her large blue eyes and dimples. However, his bear didn't react to her other than recognizing her as a friend of his sister. "What are you having to drink, or do you want to wait?"

Tiffany shook her head. "We're a little early, but I'll have a strawberry margarita."

"I'll have the same," Kaylee chimed in.

Trey watched the females for a brief moment before he rose and made his way to the bar to fill their drink orders.

He returned to the table just as Nichole and her friend joined the females. Catching Nichole's scent, his bear stood up, nudging him to move closer. His gaze locked with the raven-haired goddess's green stare. Raking his gaze over her body and drinking in her curves, he smiled and sat the drinks on the table before extending his hand to her. "Nice to see you again."

She hesitated for a moment and glanced away as if looking for an escape. He suppressed a growl, there was no need to scare the human, but he wasn't sure how long he could hold off the bear within from reaching out and touching her.

Finally, she placed her soft, warm hand in his. His body hummed with an electric charge from the connection. When she spoke quietly, he almost groaned at the sound.

"Yes, it is."

He stepped closer, still holding onto her hand. "Do you have a name?"

Even though Tiffany had told him earlier that day, he wanted his female to tell him herself.

Her brows dipped and a hint of uncertainty leaked into her cool, berry scent. Shaking his head to clear it, he released her hand and stuffed his own into the front pockets of his jeans. "I'm sorry. That was bold. Can I get you something to drink?" *Or take you home with me?*

Tiffany cleared her throat. "Nichole, this is one of my brothers. Pay him no mind."

Nichole laughed nervously and slid into the booth across from his sister. Trey's palms itched and his jeans suddenly felt way too tight.

"A rum and diet coke, please," Nichole said while averting her gaze.

He glanced to her friend. "What would you like?"

She pointed to Tiffany's drink and said, "Whatever she's having."

"Oh, get us a sampler platter, too," Tiffany added before motioning for him to leave.

He chuckled as he left the table, sneaking a quick glance back at Nichole. *Mine*, the bear snarled, not at all happy to leave the female.

Standing at the bar waiting for Donovan to fill the drink orders, Trey couldn't get the female out of his mind. Her smile lit up the room and her curves begged for his caress. Perfect in every way. And she was his mate. He was sure of it.

"Earth calling Trey."

Snapping out of his lust-induced trance, he blinked at Donovan. "Sorry."

The bear Elder nodded toward Nichole. "Be a hundred percent sure before you go spilling secrets."

Stunned, Trey stood there staring at the other bear as he moved to the end of the bar. How the fuck did the old bear do it? He always knew things. It was like he was psychic or something. However, Trey had heard that the bear had no special gifts.

When Trey turned, he came face-to-face with a highly annoyed little sister. "You are not hanging out with us. This is a girls' night. Girls. No males."

He chuckled and leaned toward her. "She's

mine. You know better than to try and stop a male from pursuing his mate."

"She doesn't need a male around."

"I'll be the judge of that."

She pursed her lips before releasing a sigh. "Damn it. Why does it have to be my friend?"

Straightening, he shrugged. "Think of it this way. You won't have to stop being her friend in ten years when it becomes obvious you're not aging."

He advanced to the table, leaving his sister at the bar. Nichole was his, and he was going to do everything in his power to make sure she accepted him and his bear. Which meant gaining her trust and love.

3

He was huge and intense. It was the only way Nichole could describe Trey. He was also sculpted to please women with his large arms, hands, thighs, and... other things hidden from view. However, his take-charge attitude told her he wasn't used to being told no. With a body like his, she didn't think he heard the word too often.

Sipping on her third rum and coke, she tried to ignore the strange electrifying heat running over her skin each time he bumped into her. The fact that he had dismissed her request for diet coke didn't slip her notice either. Add stubborn to the short description.

"Where do you work?"

Shit. Glancing to the dance floor at her friends, she sighed. "I'm in-between jobs right now."

"What *did* you do for work?"

"Bookkeeping for my ex's company."

Trey fell silent, and from the corner of her eyes, she saw the muscle in his jaw flex. But it disappeared in a flash as he turned in his seat to face her. "Donovan, the owner of this place is looking for a bookkeeper. I could set up an interview if you'd like."

Glee at having her own money again filled her. She'd been looking for months with no luck. "You don't have to do that."

He grabbed her hand, stopping her from saying anything else. Her heart pounded in her throat. Gently, he laced his fingers with hers. "Let me, please."

Well, well. He does know how to ask. Although the word *please* had come out like a seductive caress. His blue gaze mesmerized her and she knew she had been right. He didn't hear no often, because who could say no to those eyes?

No, no. She couldn't fall for anyone. Not yet. But she did need a job. "All right. Thank you."

He smiled, and she was glad to be sitting. A wash of warmth rushed through her, increasing her pulse. Her gaze fell to his sensual, kissable lips. When he lifted his hand to brush his knuckle over her cheek, she drew away. His gaze darkened and his forehead creased as if he were hurt by her reaction. Guilt tightened her chest. She knew too well what rejection felt like.

"Look, I'm sorry. I didn't mean to—"

A single finger pressed to her lips as his smile returned. "I like you, Nichole, and I want to know everything about you."

"Why?" she whispered against his finger, which was tracing her lips in a feather-like, erotic way.

He hesitated for a moment, his gaze locked with hers. "You're beautiful."

So, either he was desperate to get laid or he suffered from vision impairment. "Thank you, but I believe you're just being nice."

Sadness threatened to grab her by the throat, but she took deep breaths in hopes of chasing the emotion away. Scanning the dance floor, she panicked when she didn't see her friends. *Okay, Nichole, you need to calm the fuck down.*

Trey narrowed his gaze on her, then turned toward the dance floor. When he returned his attention to her, he brought her hand to his mouth. His soft, warm lips brushed her knuckles and send a hot wave of desire straight to her pussy. She fought to keep the moan from escaping.

What the hell was going on? She didn't even know him, yet she wanted to fuck him.

And why was she hesitating? The whole point of going out was to forget her asshole ex. So what if she had a one-night stand. She was an adult and single. Morning-afters were meant for regrets. She'd rather have a wonderful, blissful memory to go with that regret as she nursed a hangover and felt sorry for herself.

Tonight. She was going to live.

Meeting Trey's intense stare, she relaxed and offered him what she hoped was a sexy smile. "You want to get out of here?"

His lips twitched and one brow rose. "What do you have in mind?"

The fuck if she knew. Sex? Yes, sex with the hottie next to her. By the bulge in his jeans, it was on his mind, as well. "Let's go somewhere quiet."

With a short nod, he stood and offered her his hand. Chewing her bottom lip, she took it and scooted to the edge of the seat. Her stomach knotted while the rest of her body trembled. She was actually going through with it.

With a firm grip, he tugged her to a stand hard enough that she lost her footing and stumbled into him. He snaked one large arm around her and drew her closer to him. Their bodies pressed together. Desire consumed her, hot and needy.

Her heart pounded under his blue stare and she felt like she was a rabbit caught by a predator.

"I don't normally do this," she rushed out.

He caressed her cheek, his fingers slightly rough as if he worked with his hands. "Do what?"

The question came out like a husky growl that made her pulse increase and her pussy ache for his touch. "Leave with strangers."

A wicked smile curved his lips. "We're not strangers. We met this morning."

Oh, damn. The promise of passion and complete bliss floated on his words. "We should hurry before I lose my nerve."

"Hey, where are you two off to?" Connie said as she returned to the table, a little out of breath from dancing.

Nichole's cheeks heated, but it was Trey who answered. "Somewhere more private."

That sounded naughtier than it was meant to.

Nichole gently bit her lower lip as Tiffany joined them. She cast her brother a narrowed gaze before giving her attention to Nichole. "You okay?"

Nodding, Nichole rolled the hem of her sweater between her thumb and forefinger. "It was my idea."

Tiffany smiled. "Well, then. Have fun." Turning to her brother, she said, "I'll have

Donovan take us home if we get too drunk to drive."

Trey nodded and led Nichole through the crowd and out the door. Outside, she let out a breath and reminded herself that she was an adult. Sleeping with a man she'd just met was normal. Right?

Facing him, she let go of his hand and hugged her middle. "I'm sorry, I don't think I can do this."

He cupped her chin and lifted it so she could meet his blue gaze. A spark of energy passed between them, raw and hot. Her nervousness eased a fraction as she lost herself in the intensity of his desire-filled stare. Reaching up, she cupped his stubbled cheek, the course surface tingling her palm. His skin was slightly warmer than hers.

Dipping his head, he pressed his lips to hers, sending a shiver of need rolling over her. Warmth spread to her belly and lower. A wildness lingered in the taste of him, earthy with a note of cinnamon. A soft moan escaped her as he broke the kiss to scatter tiny bites along her cheek to her jawline.

"You are beautiful and deserve to be shown that," he whispered before lifting his head. "I will not do anything you don't want."

She scanned his face, searching for a hint of a lie, but she couldn't find it. Confusion clouded her mind. "I don't understand what I did to gain your attention."

He didn't reply. Instead, he gave her a sexy one-sided smile and pulled her across the parking lot to a black Jeep. After helping her into the passenger side, he climbed in the driver seat. "Where to?"

Her mind went blank. "I'm not sure."

"How about ice cream?"

"Oh, I don't—"

"Do you have food allergies? Or lactose intolerance?"

A burst of laughter rushed from her lips. He stared at her, brows drawn together. "No. Ice cream has a lot of calories and I don't need the extra."

He pursed his lips and turned in his seat to face her. "Okay, I was going to try the nice guy thing, but I can't do it. I have to be upfront with you."

Her heart sank. Just her luck she would get dumped on a one-night stand before they'd even had sex. She was pathetic. Holding one hand up, she gripped the door handle with the other. "Please, spare me the excuses. I didn't expect anything beyond tonight. I know I'm overweight and less than perfect."

Do not cry, damn it. Her eyes stung and a lump stuck in her throat as she opened the door and slid out. By the time her feet touched the asphalt, Trey was there, blocking her escape. How the hell had he gotten around the Jeep so fast?

A growl rumbled from him. "You didn't let me finish." He lifted her chin with his fingers once more and held her gaze. "I don't do one-nighters. *Ever*. And I never lie, it's a waste of my time and yours."

A little part of her believed him, but experience with jerk-offs who only wanted sex or a free ride had taught her that no man could be trusted. It all ended the same. They'd run off with the first perfect size three who gave them the time of day.

She opened her mouth, then closed it, not fully understanding what Trey was saying.

He brushed his thumb over her bottom lip. "You're perfect to me. I love your curves, your eyes, your scent."

Leaning in to her, he inhaled right before nipping her ear. She squeaked in surprise, then moaned as he sucked on her lobe.

Drawing back, he stared with a frown. "You don't believe me."

She shook her head and sagged. "Sorry. I just got out of a long-term relationship built on lies. It's hard to believe someone I just met."

"Fair enough." He stepped away a few inches,

his sexy smile lighting up his features. "Will you let me show you I'm not a lying jerk?"

"Yes, I will."

He kissed her forehead. "Good, now how about that ice cream?"

4

Trey sat across from Nichole in a corner booth at a local ice cream shop several miles outside of his den. Her shy smile around each bite was too damn cute. He'd compromised with her to get a medium sized cup, promising he'd finish whatever she didn't eat. Why did females always worry about how much they ate? Especially human females.

"You have any hobbies?" he asked, watching her pink tongue lick a drop of ice cream from her lip. The urge to lick it for her nudged him. Just the thought of it made him impossibly hard.

Her green eyes locked with his for a brief moment before she answered. "I like to read and paint."

He leaned forward, his interests lifting. She was

an artist. Why wasn't he surprised? "What do you paint?"

She shrugged. "Whatever comes to me. My favorite subjects are animals. Connie and I went hiking last summer and we got some cool pictures of some bears playing that I want to paint."

A spike of concern rose within him. "Where at?"

"We drove along Highway 2 for several miles until we found a trail we liked. I'm not sure I could ever find it again. I'm not good with directions." She laughed and glanced at her ice cream.

His Pack's land extended to the highway she'd mentioned. However, they weren't the only black bears living there. "You should be careful. Mama bears are very protective."

"Yes, the park rangers warned us. Connie has a professional-grade camera with a large lens. She takes the pictures and I paint them." Her smile spread to her eyes, making the green sparkle.

"I'd love to see your paintings someday." He covered her hand with his and lightly stroked her knuckles.

She averted her gaze, studying her melting ice cream. After a moment, she asked, "What about you? Any hobbies?"

"Getting into trouble. It's a gift."

A laugh burst from her, beautiful and song-like. He decided from that point forward he'd keep her laughing. "I'm serious. Sometimes I don't even need to be in the area and I get blamed for things."

"Are you the youngest?"

He shook his head. "The youngest son, but Tiffany is the baby. We have two older brothers."

"Wow, that's a pretty big family."

"My parents came from a big family." It wasn't a lie. The whole den was considered family. Besides, his father was the oldest of seven. Alpha families were known to be big.

She seemed to accept his answer and relaxed against the back of her seat. "When you're not getting into trouble, what do you like to do?"

"I love music. My brothers and I usually get together on weekends with a few friends and jam out." He smiled as her eyes grew round.

"You're in a band?"

"Not officially. It's just a family thing we do for fun."

She set her spoon down and pushed the cup toward him. "I'd love to see you play sometime."

Lacing his fingers with hers, he brought them to his mouth. "You can. Tomorrow night."

"It's a date." She frowned briefly, then smiled as if she liked the idea. He liked it, too. And so did his bear.

"Yes, a date." His bear growled. The beast didn't want to wait, he wanted to claim her right then. But they couldn't. It was all about trust and security with Nichole. From what Tiffany had said, Nichole had been let down and hurt too many times. Tiffany was still texting him warnings as she learned things from Connie.

Trey had turned his phone off ten minutes ago. His sister annoyed him with her matchmaking advice.

Nichole yawned, then looked at her phone. "Oh, wow. It's late."

He sighed and stood, picking up their trash. "I'll drive you home."

She silently followed him to the door and waited for him to discard the cups. His bear pawed at him, not liking the sudden mood change. The man agreed. Once they were at the Jeep, he gripped her elbow. She lifted her gaze to his and he frowned. "What is it?"

Sagging against the Jeep, she sighed. "I don't want to go home."

"Why not?"

One shoulder lifted in a half shrug. "Because Connie will most likely bring someone home, or want to stay up talking about all the fun she had dancing and all the guys she met. I love her like a sister, and any other time I'd be on board with it, but I'm just not in the mood tonight."

"You want your own story to tell." He couldn't hold his amusement in.

"Yes. Does that make me a terrible friend?"

"No, it makes you human. Someone who just broke up with her boyfriend and misses the connection." He had to take a deep breath to keep his bear from surfacing. The jerk who'd hurt her better hope they never met.

Lifting her chin with his finger, he kissed her and let his lips linger on hers for a brief moment. "You can stay at my place tonight. No sex. Unless you want to." He waggled his brows, drawing a laugh from her.

"Are you sure it's no trouble?"

He almost laughed. If she only knew the storm he battled inside himself to keep from taking her in the back seat of his Jeep. No, Nichole needed their first time to be more than a fuck in the Dairy Queen parking lot. "No trouble. I live alone, mostly. Besides,

I'm a male. Any way I can get you closer to my bed, the better."

She smiled and shoved at him playfully before she turned to open the door. He beat her to it and helped her into the seat. When he met her stare, he lifted a brow. "What?"

"All this nice-guy act will stop as soon as you get me into bed, won't it?" The spark in her eyes told him she was teasing.

Nipping at her nose, he said, "Of course. What kind of male do you think I am?"

A breathless laugh escaped and she shoved him before closing the door. Shaking his head with a happiness he hadn't felt in a long time, he climbed in the driver's side and pulled out of the parking lot.

Her nervousness drifted around him in a bouquet of ice and berries, enticing the bear. Glancing at her hands, he sighed and covered her fidgeting fingers with his own. She relaxed a little, but her scent was still strong and drugging. His own relief came when he turned off Highway 2 onto a narrow road that led deep into the Cohutta Wilderness Area.

Another ten minutes and he'd be home.

All he had to do was tell her about his ability to

shift into a large black bear and hope she didn't freak out and run.

He would have to chase her down because his bear wouldn't take no for an answer.

5

She had gone crazy. Her belly had a thousand butterflies fighting for space. And it didn't escape her notice that he had driven into the mountains, where, according to maps, there were no houses. *Calm down, Nichole.*

She opened her mouth to ask where they were going when he pulled into a narrow, dirt driveway. Waiting to see where they ended up, she held her tongue. It was too late anyway. There was no way she'd be able to outrun him.

God, she should have taken self-defense classes with Connie.

A few moments later, they pulled to a stop in front of a modest size cabin with a wraparound porch. From the Jeep's headlights, she noticed the rose bushes that lined the front of the porch and brightened it with red, pink, yellow, and lavender blooms.

"Oh, this is nice." She opened the door and climbed out.

"Thank you," he said a moment later, coming up behind her. With his lips next to her ear, he whispered, "I'm not going to hurt you."

She whirled around. "I didn't...know there were homes out here."

He let out a soft chuckle. "My family and I like our privacy."

"Well, there's nothing more private than out here." She couldn't wait to see what it looked like in the morning. "It's so peaceful."

"And beautiful."

Yes. It was.

He took her hand and led her inside the cabin. The light flicked on and she blinked to adjust her sight. She crossed the oak, hardwood floors to the living room. A black leather sofa and two matching chairs sat in a semi-circle in front of a large flat-screen TV.

"You said earlier that you *mostly* live alone. What did you mean?"

He frowned. "My brothers like to pop in without calling or knocking. So don't be alarmed if they do it when you're here."

Shyness made her avert her gaze from him. He'd begun speaking like they were a couple and would be for awhile. Which was crazy. They'd just met. Although, she had felt a connection grow between them, getting stronger the more time they spent together. It was one reason she didn't want to go home. She didn't understand it and hoped to figure it out, or have him tell her why.

No matter how nice he was to her, she couldn't shake the feeling he was hiding something from her. She needed to know what it was before she slept with him or gave him her heart.

Where the hell had that come from?

"Are you okay?"

"Huh? Oh, yeah. Fine." She forced a smile and sat on the sofa.

"That doesn't sound too convincing."

Staring at him, she gathered her courage into a ball and clung to it. "What are you not telling me? I can tell there's something. And why do I feel a connection to you? It's like we've known each other for a lifetime, when we really just met."

He squeezed his eyes shut and sat on the coffee table in front of her. When he opened them, his gaze seemed to glow. "Do you believe in love at first sight?"

She shook her head. "There was a time I did. Experience has taught me better."

"Well, I do. At least I believe there is a fated mate out there for me. You're her."

Fated mate? What an odd way to phrase it. "I don't understand."

He scooted forward and cradled her hands. "What I'm about to tell you can't be repeated. My safety, as well as that of my family, depends on it."

She swallowed and nodded. His forehead creased and the blue of his irises darkened. A shimmer rolled through his gaze, reminding her of Connie when she performed a power spell. Curious, Nichole opened her mind like her friend had taught her and searched for Trey's magickal signature. What she found was something different altogether.

"What animal are you?" she asked, searching his gaze.

His eyes grew round and his grip on her hands tightened. "How do you know?'

Offering him a smile, she averted her gaze. "Connie taught me to read auras. I'm not a witch, but she says I have a bit of magick in me."

When he didn't answer right away, she lifted her

gaze to his. He relaxed. "Bear. I'm a bear. I was dreading your reaction and wasn't sure how or when to tell you."

"I've known since I met Connie that she was a witch, but only recently found out about shifters. I'm not sure how I feel about it." She frowned.

A bear shifter.

She knew nothing about bears, other than to stay out of their way. But that was the wild ones. His earlier words about finding a mate entered her mind. Oh, no. She couldn't mate a bear.

Fumbling with her tote, she scrambled from the sofa and rushed to the door. "I'm sorry. I can't do this."

He was in front of her before she took her second step. "Yes, you can. I can smell your desire for me."

She scanned his home and was reminded that she was in the middle of nowhere, completely at his mercy. As if picking up on her unease, he held out his hand, palm up. "Please, let me explain."

There was that damn, soft plea again. *Damn.* What choice did she have, really? She could call Connie, but she was most likely drunk and unable to drive. Defeat settled over her and she placed her hand in his. "Okay."

His eyes brightened slightly as he linked their

fingers and tugged her back to sit on the sofa. Before she sat, he cradled her face. "Spend the next twenty-four hours with me. If I can't seduce you into agreeing to the mating, then I'll let you go and never bother you again."

The last few words were said with a low growl before his features darkened and he lowered his gaze. Her chest tightened. She could almost feel his sorrow as her own, but how? "Okay, but I get twenty-four hours after that to think about it."

He raised his lashes and the corner of his lips lifted. "Deal."

Sinking down on the sofa, she let out a breath. Why did it feel like she'd just signed her soul away to a bear?

∼

"What's going on in that head of yours?" Trey kept his tone light. He could still sense Nichole's need to flee.

She locked gazes with him and smiled. Although he could tell it was forced. Damn, he wished he knew what to do to help her relax. "You don't want to know. It's a scary place."

At least she still teased him. Good. He'd go with it.

"Not scarier than mine."

Her brows bunched. *Fuck. Good one, jerk. Remind her you're an animal.* "I'm sorry."

"Don't be. I..." She shook her head. "I'm just trying to process it all. Can I ask you some questions?"

"Anything. Are you thirsty? Hungry?"

She let out a soft laugh. "After that ice cream, I can't possibly eat anything else. What do you have to drink?"

He gave a short nod and walked to the kitchen. When was the last time he'd gone shopping? Opening the fridge, he frowned. "I have beer, water, and milk." He glanced at the date on the carton, then threw the thing in the trash. "Scratch the milk."

Her light laugh reached his ears, making him smile. "Beer is fine."

A woman after his own heart. He picked up two long-necks and went back to the living room. Taking a seat next to her on the sofa, he removed the cap to one of the beers before handing it to her. "What would you like to know about me?"

She studied her beer and picked at the label. "I'm not sure where to begin."

He sat back and propped his feet up on the coffee table. "Well, I'm a black bear. Shifters tend to be a little larger than the non-shifting animals. We don't have to hibernate in the winter because we are actually humans with an animal soul. No, that sounds odd."

That got a giggle out of her. "The way Connie explained it, shifters are from magickal bloodlines like witches, but are a separate species from human and witches. They are one with their animal spirits, and shifting is a natural part of life."

"That's a pretty good description. Although there are some differences from Pack to Pack."

Her head bobbed and her black hair swayed. He reached out and brushed the ends, feeling the silky strands against his fingers.

"That makes sense. Even witches have different powers and beliefs." She glanced at him and smiled.

The tip of her pink tongue swiped over her bottom lip. He tracked the movement and without a conscious thought, leaned forward and crushed his mouth to hers. Passion overrode all forms of caution as he thrust his tongue into her mouth, searching for hers.

She moaned into the kiss and wrapped her arms around his neck, drawing their bodies closer. A low growl escaped him. Awareness of her seeped into every pore of his body—her scent, her nearness, the heat of her skin.

Mine.

Yes, he agreed with the bear. Nichole was theirs.

With another low, soft growl, he tore his mouth away from hers and trailed light kisses down her jaw to her throat. Her breath came in short pants as she clung to his shoulders, scoring his skin through the thin cotton of his T-shirt with her nails.

Clamping down his jaw to keep from biting her, he tightened his hold. "If you want me to stop, now is the time to say so."

"It's crazy, but I don't want you to stop. I ache everywhere. Is this normal?"

He inhaled her cool, berry scent, then kissed her nose. "Perfectly normal when you've met your mate."

Uncertainty darkened her gaze. He pressed his lips to hers, keeping her from denying the mating. Her scent betrayed her. The slight musk mixed in her natural scent said she was more than ready for him to take her, to pleasure her until she screamed his name.

"The first thing you will learn, is that you are

beautiful." He stood, lifting her with him and carrying her to his bedroom.

After laying her on the king size bed, he hovered over her. "One thing about bears is..." A kiss to her forehead. "...we love beautiful, curvy women." He kissed her nose, then her lips before adding, "Plus, we mate for life."

Her eyes widened as her lips curved into a sensual smile. "So, you will spoil me until the end of our lives?"

Whether she knew it or not, she had accepted him. At least a small part of her had. "Every day we have together." He pressed a finger to her lips. "Now stop thinking and just enjoy the moment."

He moved to the end of the bed and slipped her shoes off, then crawled on the bed between her legs. With a quick jerk, he removed her tight, black jeans, taking her panties with them. A half groan, half growl rumbled in his throat.

Her green gaze locked with his, watching him. Without breaking the eye contact, he sank down between her legs and nudged her thighs apart. When he spread her lips, she sucked in a breath. "So wet."

He licked from her entrance to her clit, savoring her sweet taste. His dick pressed painfully into the zipper of his jeans. Nichole closed her eyes, and he covered her sex with his mouth, sucking and teasing. Pleasure rolled through him with each pleasured moan she released.

Slipping two fingers inside her hot, wet pussy, he flicked his tongue over the bundle of sensitive nerves. Her hips moved in time with his thrusts and licks, telling him what she wanted. Picking up the tempo, he replaced his tongue with his thumb so he could watch her when she came.

"Come for me, baby."

A scream ripped from her as the orgasm slammed into her and her body spasmed while her pussy squeezed his fingers.

Good, gods, she was gorgeous when she came.

∽

NICHOLE SMILED like she had never done before. If she thought she'd had orgasms before, then she didn't know what to call what she'd just had. And Trey hadn't even had sex with her yet.

"You okay?"

She nodded, not trusting her voice to work.

His handsome, rugged face appeared in her line of sight, and her heart skipped a couple of beats. She cupped his cheek and smiled. "You have a very talented tongue."

A laugh burst from him before he nipped at her chin. "You taste divine."

When she went to shake her head, he kissed her, hard and deep. Hunger rose within her again, building into a throbbing need to have him inside her. She tangled her tongue with his, tasting herself.

Snaking an arm around her, he lifted her up and removed her sweater. With quick efficiency, her bra went next. The *swish* of clothing falling to the floor faded away when he flicked his tongue over one nipple.

Heat coiled in her belly, spreading throughout her body. Damn. The man was going to break her. No, he was going to ruin her for all others.

"Trey."

The single word came out needy, but she didn't care. She wanted him inside her. *Now*.

With a soft growl, he stood and removed his clothes. Hunger lit up his blue gaze, intensifying her own. When he positioned his cock to her entrance, she pressed a hand to his chest. "Wait."

A sensual smile lifted his lips. "I can't carry human diseases, and you're not ovulating."

She frowned. "You can't? I'm not? How can you tell?"

"When females ovulate, their scent changes. It's sweeter."

"Oh." She suppressed the urge to smell herself. *Nichole, you're being silly.*

"I can wear a condom if it makes you feel better."

She stared at him. Concern laced with mischief danced in his gaze. She'd bet he didn't even have a condom. Really, did it matter? She trusted him. Somehow, in the short few hours she'd known him, he'd gained her trust and started to wiggle his way into her heart.

"No, you don't have to wear one."

The blue in his eyes darkened, then shimmered. He nipped at her bottom lip as he thrust inside her, drawing a gasp from her. She fisted the sheet and dug her heels into the mattress. Pleasure raced through her veins and straight to her core, building.

His body tensed just as her release exploded, dragging her over the edge. His orgasm followed, his hot seed spilling inside her.

Trey collapsed beside her and gathered her close. His heart beat frantically in her ear. She smiled and snuggled into him. "That was..."

"Amazing," he finished her thought.

Laughing, she kissed his chest before releasing a sigh. "Yes."

"We should really get up and shower."

She nodded. "I know, but I don't want to move."

Without warning, he got out of bed and lifted her into his arms to carry her to the bathroom. He set her on her feet and turned on the shower. Cocking her head to the side, she watched him, admiring his large, muscular backside.

He straightened and slowly turned to face her, a wide smile brightening his features. "Like what you see."

A giggle bubbled up and she averted her gaze. Heat filled her cheeks and she could only imagine that they were bright red.

A moment later, Trey had his arms around her waist and his mouth on hers. A sigh slipped through her lips when he lifted his head to stare into her eyes. "I like it when you look at me with that fire of yours."

"I'm in trouble."

"Why?"

"My heart is in jeopardy of being broken."

His brows dipped and he caressed her cheek. "Not by me. Remember, bears mate for life."

Yeah, but humans didn't. What if she didn't want this in a few years?

And why was she thinking about the future already?

Because Trey had wiggled his way into her heart. It didn't make any sense.

"Don't fight what is fated to be," he whispered a moment before he scooped her up and entered the shower.

Warm water cascaded over both of them. Trey lowered her to her feet and kissed her briefly. "I'll go as slow as you need me to. Just promise not to walk away from me until you understand fully what it means to mate with a bear."

6

Nichole woke, confused for a moment at where she was. Images of the night before filled her thoughts and she warmed. Trey had given her passion beyond her wildest dreams. He was everything she'd ever wished for in a boyfriend. With a smile, she rose from the bed and stretched, her muscles aching in all the right places.

She walked to the bedroom door and opened it. Hushed voices drifted down the hall. Drawing her brows together, she advanced toward the living room. A large man who looked a lot like Trey sat on the sofa, his stern glare pinning her as she entered the room, forcing her to take a step back.

She recognized him from the café the day before.

Trey turned to her and held out his hand. "Come here, Nichole. Please."

Hesitantly, she moved forward and allowed him to pull her into his lap. His warmth enveloped her in a tight, soothing embrace.

"This is my oldest brother, Anthony." Trey had a hint of a growl in his words. It was like he didn't want his brother there.

Meeting Anthony's hard stare, she offered a smile. He nodded in return and said, "Good morning."

"Morning." She kept her tone low. The man across from her held a power she'd never felt before. A voice in her head said to keep her distance.

As if sensing her uneasiness, Trey linked his fingers with hers. Instantly, she relaxed.

Anthony's gaze locked onto their linked hands a moment before he raised his eyes to hers. "Secrecy is very important for us."

"Yes, I know. My best friend is a witch. She's told me a little about shifters."

He raised a brow. "Like what?"

Her pulse raced and she fumbled over her words. "I...she just told me you exist and to stay clear."

A bitter laugh escaped Anthony. "And here you are, the mate of a bear."

"I haven't agreed to mate with your brother."

Trey squeezed her gently. "But I'm working on it."

Her cheeks heated and she glanced down at their linked hands. What did it mean to be mated to a shifter? Especially a bear.

Anthony stood. "Come to dinner with the family tonight."

When he left, Trey let out a soft growl, startling Nichole. "Sorry, Ant can be an ass."

"He has a lot of power surrounding him."

"He's the Marshal of the clan. It's his job to see that the laws are enforced and ensure that the den is safe." Trey patted her on the bottom as if he wanted her to get up.

She stood and stepped aside when he did the same. "It makes sense now. He came by to make sure I'm not a threat."

The muscles in Trey's jaw flexed. "He should have better faith in my judgment."

She felt a smile tug at her lips. "He worries about you."

Trey shrugged and led the way to the kitchen, stopping at the breakfast nook. "Have a seat, I'll fix you breakfast. What would you like?"

"I guess fruit and yogurt is out."

He rolled his eyes and turned to the fridge. "Yep.

How about cinnamon French toast with a strawberry syrup."

"Sounds amazing."

His lips curved. "Good, because it's what Tiffany dropped off right before Ant stopped by."

Nichole laughed. "I guess it's a good thing I can cook."

"Hey, I can cook."

"Really? Like what?"

"Cereal and mac and cheese."

She held in another laugh. "Oh, we're living it up. Do you need help warming up the French toast?"

He glanced at her, a playful gleam in his eyes. "I do know how to work the microwave, female."

Pressing her lips together to keep from smiling, she watched him move around the kitchen. His shoulders flexed and bunched as he pulled plates from the cupboards. Suddenly, he stilled and looked at her. "Where are you from?"

"I was born in Jacksonville, Florida. My dad was in the Army, so we moved a lot."

He went back to fixing the plates and placed them in the microwave. "That must have been hard."

She shrugged. "It was part of my life."

"Where are your parents now?"

Her stomach dropped. She really didn't want to talk about them. "They retired in Florida."

The microwave dinged. He removed the plates and hooked his pinky through the handle of the syrup bottle from Beary Sweets. When he sat the items on the table and took his seat, he poured her syrup until she said when to stop.

"By your tone, I take it you aren't close."

"I'm not the picture-perfect daughter they'd hoped for."

He grunted before taking a bite. Once he finished chewing, he asked, "In what way?"

"My best friend practices witchcraft, and I refuse to marry the man they picked out for me."

His gaze locked with hers. The blue in his eyes darkened. "You're betrothed?"

Shaking her head, she fought the urge to reach for him to comfort the bear within. "No. There is no contract. Thank God. Besides, the guy married someone else when I turned him down. I think he was relieved I had the guts to say no."

"Sounds like a winner with no backbone."

She snorted, which made the both of them laugh. "He was kind of a nerd, but smart, sweet, and cute. He had a bright future ahead of him. I just didn't feel the fire."

Not like the one she felt with Trey. In fact, no one had sparked a flame in her like the bear shifter in front of her had.

"What about you? Have you always lived here?"

He nodded, and she was glad he allowed her to switch the subject back to him. "All my life. My dad is the Alpha of the clan. You met Anthony. I have one other brother, Ryan, who is the Beta. He looks after the needs of the clan and deals with conflicts."

"Like sibling rivalries?"

"Yeah. The clan is one big family."

She scooted the last few bites around her plate. She had always wanted a large family, and now it appeared she had one if she wanted it. How could she commit to someone she'd met less than a day ago though?

He reached across the table and covered her hand. "I want to show you the den."

Smiling, she held his gaze. "I'd like that."

His sensual mouth lifted in a brilliant smile, warming her to the core. Releasing her hand, he rose from his seat and moved to her side. His fingers were warm as they brushed her cheek. Tingles skittered over her skin. Lifting her chin, he dipped his head and pressed his lips to hers. The flame flared to life, threatening to consume her like a wildfire.

Too soon, he broke the kiss, picked up her plate and walked to the sink.

Damn, she was confused.

She wanted him more and more each moment they spent together. It was crazy. Wasn't it?

∾

Trey loved having his mate by his side and in his den. However, he could sense her battling her own feelings. He wished there was something he could do to make her decision easier, but there wasn't. Nichole had to make her choice, and he would live with whatever decision she made.

One thing he *could* do was make her day with him the best she'd ever had.

"Trey?"

"Yes."

"Tell me about mating."

He took a deep breath and exhaled slowly. "Many believe mates are chosen by the Fates. Although we can complete the mating with anyone."

"Wouldn't it be better with your fated mate?"

"Of course." He squeezed her hand slightly.

"How do you know when you've met your fated mate?"

He stopped and faced her. "For me, it's your scent that sparks the bear's interest. And the sound of your voice is soothing in a way I've never experienced."

Her heart rate increased as he closed the small gap between them.

"What are some signs I should look for, for me?"

Cupping her cheek, he pressed his forehead to hers. His bear puffed out his chest at Nichole's soft sigh at their connection. "A draw, a feeling of belonging, I guess. It's what I've felt since seeing you at Tiffany's bakery."

The smell of peaches drifted around them, drawing a smile from him. Pulling away from Nichole, he turned to his mother. "Nichole, meet my mom, Madison."

"I began to wonder if my son was keeping you all to himself. Tiffany has chattered about you all morning. I had to come over and meet you." Trey's mom's pale blue eyes sparkled with interest as she studied Nichole.

Trey cleared his throat. "I didn't want to scare her away so soon."

Madison waved a hand at him and linked an arm

with Nichole. "Males are all the same. But they can't help it. It's in their nature to be protectors."

Nichole smiled wide. "So, if Trey's father is Alpha, does that make you mama bear?"

A song-like laugh escaped his mother. "Yes, it does." She paused as if a thought had entered her mind. "I like you. You have a good soul and an open mind."

Trey's chest tightened at his mother's acceptance of his mate. It was no easy task to win over Madison Black, but Nichole had done it in a few moments.

"Mom!" Tiffany rushed to them, her eyes round. "Jack is gone. I turned my head for a second, and he's gone!"

Their mother let out a sigh and released Nichole's arm. "Come, Nichole. I'll show you how to hunt down a mischievous bear cub."

7

Nichole followed Madison and Tiffany toward the center of town where they took a right at what looked like a school. All the while, Tiffany wrung her hands and shook her head.

"His parents will never trust me with him again. I'm going to make a terrible mother."

"I wouldn't judge your parenting skills by Jack. He's an escape artist," Trey said as he trailed behind them.

Madison smiled. "Your brother is right, dear. Don't worry, we'll find the little monster."

Hiding her smile, Nichole dipped her head. Her mother used to call the neighbor kids little monsters when they got into trouble. The memory made her nose tingle. She pushed the unwanted feelings away and took a deep breath. She would not feel sorrow for a woman who had turned her away at age seventeen.

Trey's warm hand cupped her nape as he tucked her into his side. "What is it?"

She shook her head but couldn't form the words to tell him it was nothing. Luckily, the women stopped at the edge of the forest.

Madison held up a hand and spoke to Tiffany. "What do you smell?"

Tiffany sniffed the air. Out of curiosity, so did Nichole. To her surprise, she smelled the faint scent of honey. When she closed her eyes and focused her second sight out, she heard a child's laugh and the trickling of water.

Flinging her eyes open, she met Trey's stare. "Is there water nearby?"

"Yes."

Without thinking, she took off in the direction of where she hoped Jack was. Her heart pounded with worry for the young boy. It didn't take her long to reach a small stream. However, what stood in the middle of it was not a little boy. Instead, a small black bear cub splashed through the water.

Trey stopped beside her and started laughing before he marched into the water and picked the cub up by the scruff of his neck. "Cousin Tif was very worried about you."

He thumped the cub on the nose, making the little guy sneeze.

Tiffany walked over and took the bear from her brother. "You are so bad." She met Nichole's gaze and smiled. "How did you know?"

"I'm not sure. I focused on finding him and heard water. I was so scared he'd drown. I totally forgot how well bears can swim."

Madison stroked her fingers through Jack's fur. "It is possible that you have a witch or two in your bloodline. Or that you are one of the sensitive humans."

Nichole considered it. She'd have to research her family tree to see if Madison were right.

"Come on, we have a tour to finish." Trey took her hand and tugged her back to the den.

Madison called out, "Don't be late for dinner."

"We won't," Trey answered.

Nichole smiled from ear to ear. The love between him and his mother reached out to her, surrounding her in warm energy. "I like your mom."

"She likes you. And she has great judgment in people." He wrapped an arm around her and kissed her temple.

She could get used to all the attention he gave her. But how long would it last?

~

Trey scented trouble before she rounded the corner in front of the nursery. Tall and pretty, April had always had her eye on him, but his bear would have nothing to do with her. She stalked toward them, her glare never leaving Nichole.

"Hello, April."

"Hi. Who's the human?"

Trey growled, but Nichole tightened her grip on his hand before offering her other hand to April. "Name's Nichole."

April didn't shake her hand. Instead, she glanced to Trey and smirked. "I enjoyed our time together the other night."

When she reached for him, he gripped her wrist and snarled. "I helped my brothers move furniture into your apartment. That's it." He shoved her back. *Jealous bitch.* "Nichole is my fated mate. You will show her respect."

With a gentle tug of Nichole's hand, he turned

away from the female and headed back to his home. "Please stay away from her."

"What is her problem?"

"She's jealous. One by one, my brothers have turned her down. I'm her next chase." He stopped and faced her. "April is manipulative. She likes to start trouble, and I wouldn't put it past her to tell you lies."

Nichole glanced at the female briefly, then into his eyes. "I've never understood people like that."

He shrugged. "Me neither. April wasn't born into the Pack. She moved here from the Rocky Mountains about ten years ago. Everything was great; she adjusted well to my father's law. Then we started having issues with a few of the surrounding Packs."

"What type of trouble?" Nichole's tone was curious and held a hint of concern.

His pride swelled.

"There is a shifter war going on, mainly between the big cats and wolves. My father, with the help of our Pack Elder, has worked hard to keep us out of it. Yet we are not without our own enemies." He paused and considered dropping the subject. April always found a way to get under his skin, but Nichole had a right to know.

"April invited one of our enemies into the den without the Alpha's permission. Normally, the punishment for her actions would have been to ship her back to her Pack. But April swore she didn't know that the male was our enemy, and Anthony talked Father into leniency." Trey snorted. He hadn't liked April the moment they'd met. There was just something...not right about her.

Nichole stared at him, her eyes narrowing slightly. "What else did she do?"

His mate was too intuitive at times, but Trey like that about her. "April and my mother were taking a group of young bears on their first hunt a few months ago. A one of the boys wandered off, and my mother left the group to search for him. Instead of calling her back when the boy showed up, April decided to take them back to the den."

He fisted his hands at the memory before continuing. "Mom got caught in a hunter's trap. The only reason we found her was through the mating link between my parents. Dad felt her pain and instantly went to find her."

Nichole frowned and her cheeks colored as if she were angry. "That was irresponsible of April."

"Yeah, but she swore she thought my mother was right behind her. Anthony put her on watch, warning her that the next incident would get her a ticket straight back to the Rockies." Stopping at his front door, he caressed her cheek. "Stay away from her. Don't listen to anything she tells you. Please."

Nichole leaned into his touch. "I can sense lies. Don't worry about me going near her. She's not the type of person I like to hang out with anyway."

His lips tugged into a smile. "Good. I think she's crazy."

The corners of her lips twitched, but he didn't press her to speak her mind. He'd made a promise to allow her to make her own decision. Damn, it was going to be hard to let her go think it over for a day.

8

Nichole wiped her clammy hands on her jeans and tried like hell to stop them from trembling. She was nervous. "What is your dad like?"

Trey slipped his phone into his pocket and met her gaze. With a slow sensual smile, he stepped closer to her and took her hands in his. "You have nothing to worry about."

Narrowing her gaze on him, she watched how his irises darkened slightly, although she didn't sense a lie from him. "That's not answering my question."

"He's intense on his best days but will never do anything to upset his mate."

She released a breath she didn't realize she'd been holding. "Thank you for being honest."

A chuckle rumbled from his chest and he linked their fingers together and tugged her to the door. "He also hates to be kept waiting, so we need to go. Now."

Her heart rate kicked up a few more beats per second. He stopped, faced her, and pressed his lips to hers. Heat spread within her like wildfire. He drew back and cradled her face. "He will love you. The Alpha of any Pack knows a true mating and will not stand in the way of fate."

True mating. She wished she were as sure as he was. Nodding, she smiled. "Okay. I'm calm. A little."

He smiled as he shook his head and tugged her down the dirt path toward the small village-like town in the middle of the forest.

His parents' house wasn't much bigger than Trey's. Nichole wasn't sure what she had expected. Maybe a large, elegant home? This was cozy. Red brick covered the exterior with white trim and shutters. A wraparound porch gave the home a comforting feel.

She followed Trey to the front door and entered when he opened the door. Madison was the first to greet them, drawing Nichole into a tight hug.

"Dinner is almost ready." Madison glanced at Trey, a hint of concern in her gaze. "Donovan is in the living room with your brothers and father."

Trey frowned briefly before kissing Nichole on

the cheek. When he moved toward the other room, Nichole gripped his hand. "What is it?"

"Alpha business."

Madison looped an arm with Nichole. "Come help me get the table set."

Glancing at the older woman, who didn't look a day over forty, Nichole gave a short nod and allowed Trey's mom to lead her into the kitchen.

Tiffany stood at a small island in the middle of the room with a pink apron on and flour dusting her cheeks and forehead. "Hi, Nichole."

"Hi. What are you making?"

"Truffles."

So that wasn't flour, but powdered sugar. Nichole held in a smile. "I love truffles."

"I know. Connie told me."

"What else did my witchy BFF tell you?"

A grin formed on Tiffany's face. "Lots of stuff."

"Tiffany, behave," Madison said as she handed a stack of plates to Nichole. "We're doing buffet style."

Nichole glanced to the table in the dining room through the archway on the other side of the kitchen. A few items had already been placed. With a nod, she took the plates and carried them to the table. A moment later, Trey wrapped his arms around her waist and kissed her neck.

"Don wants to meet you."

"What?" she turned in his arms and froze at the large, bearded man standing behind Trey.

"I'm Donovan. Trey says you're an accountant."

"Um, I've done some bookkeeping." She glanced to Trey.

Donovan nodded. "Good enough. Can you start on Monday?"

She opened her mouth, then closed it. Glee filled her chest. "Sure."

"Good. I'll see you at The Claw, Monday at 10:00 AM." Then the large bear moved to Madison and kissed her cheek before leaving the house.

What the hell just happened? She got a job, that's what. And would soon have her own money.

"I see my son is trying to keep you to himself." The low rumble of Trey's father's voice flowed over her like warm silk.

"Hello, Mr. Black."

One dark brow lifted a moment before a deep chuckle left his lips. "Please, call me Elijah. Then, when you make your decision, call me Dad."

Her chest tightened while a smile lifted her lips. "I will."

Trey nudged her with his shoulder, then whispered, "He's a big teddy bear."

She giggled but moved aside when Madison and Tiffany set out the rest of the food.

"Let's eat," Tiffany said with a smile. "Nichole can learn all about Trey growing up."

Laughing at Trey's scowl, Nichole played along. "That sounds fun."

∼

"You weren't joking when you said you were always in trouble."

Trey let out a low, playful growl that made his mate giggle. "My family will someday pay for embarrassing me."

Nichole hugged him tightly as they walked down the path to the stream. "Family is good like that. At least you have them."

Her voice cracked at the last statement. Coming to a stop, he turned her to face him and cradled her head. "Have you tried to reach out to your parents?"

She sighed. "Yes, about twice a year. Each time it's the same. My mother refuses to talk to me, and my dad isn't any better. He sides with her. It doesn't matter anymore. I have Connie."

Fury at how her parents had cast her out threatened to surface. He squashed it down and offered a gentle smile. "You also have my family. It's probably for the best anyway."

"What do you mean?"

He held her hand and began walking again. "When we form the bond, you'll stop aging and take my lifespan. You'd have to cut yourself out of your family's lives anyway because I don't think they'd accept you being mated to a bear."

"You're right. They wouldn't." Her mouth dipped slightly, then lifted just as quickly. "But I'm okay with it. I've been on my own for a very long time."

He leaned in and kissed her nose. "I can't imagine what it would be like to not have my parents' support. I'm sorry you don't."

Crinkling her nose up, she wrapped her arms around his neck. "I'm seriously okay with it. I learned a long time ago not to depend on them. I love who I've become."

"Even if it's a sexy, curvy girl on the mend from a broken heart?"

A laugh burst from her lips. "Yes. I was being a whiny drama queen."

Hope flooded his senses. "So you've made your choice?"

"Not so fast." She placed a finger to his lips, and he wanted to suck the digit into his mouth. "I get twenty-four hours to think about things without your charm making it impossible to think. Remember."

"That's not me, it's the bear."

Her smile widened and she rolled her eyes. "Sure, blame it on the bear."

"True story."

"Uh huh." She sucked in her bottom lip and averted her gaze. Her scent spike slightly indicating that she was nervous about something.

Studying her closer, he touched her chin with a finger, then gently turned her head toward him. "What is it?"

"I...um...Can I see him?"

His bear clawed at him in a *hell yes*, eager to meet her, to have her fingers in his fur. "Of course. Stay here."

After taking several steps away from her, he removed his shirt and jeans. Her apparent arousal as she stared at his naked form made him groan. Nudity was a natural part of life for shifters, but in front of one's mate... Well, it was hard to focus. Closing his eyes, he pushed away the urge to take her right there and called his bear.

The shift was always quick. Especially for

those descended from the Alpha bloodline. His bear surfaced, taking over his mind and body. A flash of grey and silver entered his mind right before his view of the world altered to that of the bear's.

Nichole stood frozen a few feet away, her hand over her mouth. "Wow. You are beautiful. And huge."

Trey laughed. Although to Nichole it most likely sounded like a growl. When he didn't smell fear on her, he eased closer. God he wished he could talk to her in this form. No, that talent was reserved for family only.

"Can you understand me?" she asked, then laughed. "Sorry. Of course, you can."

Amused, he continued forward until he was inches from her. Relief flooded him when she reached out and threaded her fingers through the fur on the top of his head. He nudged her hand and moved closer.

Damn if he didn't want to rub against her like a damned cat.

Unable to stand it any longer, he shifted back to human and hugged her against him. "I want to be selfish and not share you with the bear right now. My hunger for you is too strong."

Her cool hands rested on his chest. "I know. It's hard to think."

"It's the mating dance—very confusing and amazing all in one."

She drew her brows together and made small circles with her finger under his collarbone. "Your twenty-four hours is up."

He let out a sigh. "I was hoping to distract you into staying another night. But a deal is a deal. Unless…"

The moonlight kissed her face as she lifted her gaze back to his. "I'd love to stay another night, then another. Yet, I'm confused, overwhelmed, happy… I need to think."

"I know. It's going to be rough not seeing you for the next twenty-four hours, but I promised." He stepped away and took her hand. "Come on, I'll get dressed and take you home. Unless I can persuade you to stay and watch my brothers and I jam tonight."

Her eyes widened. "I think I might be persuaded."

He snaked an arm around her, drawing her closer. "Then stay one more night. I promise to wake you before the sun rises to take you home."

When she hesitated, he raised a brow. Concern rushed through him, cooling his blood. "What is it?"

"You are too good to be true."

His heart swelled with joy. "My mate deserves only the best."

Her laugh was light. She opened her mouth, then closed it. Their gazes locked for a few moments and he wondered what she was thinking. Her scent didn't betray anything other than tiredness and confusion.

"I know I told you once your twenty-four hours starts, if I didn't hear from you I'd leave you alone. I can't do that unless I hear you tell me to."

"Fair enough." She wrapped her arms around him. "Thank you."

"For what?"

"Showing me I'm beautiful and giving me an amazing day."

There are more of those days to come. He didn't say the words out loud. No, he didn't want to scare her off, or point out that she'd already made up her mind. Only she could convince herself of that.

With a gentle tug, he led her back to his house. Once she left him, the next twenty-four hours were going to be hell without her by his side. His bear was going to drive him mad.

9

Nichole sat at the small round table in her kitchen staring into her cup of tea. Connie had made it hoping it'd help relax her. It hadn't.

Sleep was impossible due to a certain sexy bear shifter haunting her thoughts. Besides, he was true to his words and woke her at 5:00 AM to drive her home. That only gave her three hours of sleep. Once she'd arrived home, going back to bed was out of the question. Her skin felt tight, and oddly enough, she felt empty, like something was missing.

"It's the mating pull," Connie said as she sat across from her. "I heard it was more powerful than any love spell a witch can weave."

Releasing a sigh, Nichole took a sip of her herbal tea. Notes of orange and cocoa coated her tongue before she swallowed. She was supposed to take the next twenty-four hours to run through the pros and cons of mating the bear her soul called to.

"How can I make a sound decision?"

Connie covered her hand and smiled. "Don't think. Pack your bags and drive your ass back to the den, throw yourself into his arms, and then say *yes*, for the love of the gods!"

It sounded so easy. "But we just met."

Sitting back in her chair, Connie folded her arms. "My parents loved each other from the moment their gazes connected. They were married three days later." She laughed before continuing. "If it is the will of the Fates, you don't really have a say in it."

A smile tugged at Nichole's mouth. Connie's parents had been married for over fifty years and acted like a couple of lovestruck teens. "Will it last?"

"What? The thrill? The heat?"

Nichole's cheeks warmed. "Yes."

"I've heard it does for as long as you live together."

"Who did you hear this from?"

Connie grinned. "My aunt was mated to a wolf. She told me the connection and love grew stronger each year of their lives together."

"You mean Robyn?"

"Yep."

Nichole frowned. She'd never known Robyn Hunter was mated. She definitely didn't know she had been mated to a wolf. "What happened to her mate?"

"He was killed by a hunter while in wolf form." Connie's brows dipped. "You want a con on mating? It's extremely painful to lose your mate, to lose the connection to one another. Aunt Robyn fell into a deep depression. It was Travis, her son, who pulled her out of it."

"Oh." They fell silent for a few moments. That was one con, but the pros still outweighed it. *Damn*. She wouldn't last the full twenty-four hours.

She sat her cup down and stood.

"Where are you going?" Connie waggled her brows.

"To get myself mated to a bear."

Her hands shook all the way to the den. She was surprised she hadn't crashed her Mini along the way. "Oh, please be home."

She pulled into Trey's driveway and her stomach flipped like it was trying out for Cirque du Soleil or something. It was a good thing she hadn't eaten yet. *Okay, Nichole, calm down. You're only gambling with the rest of your life. Oh God, help me.*

With a deep breath, she shut off the engine, got out of the car, and ran to the house. When she reached the porch, the front door opened, but it wasn't Trey who stood there.

"April."

It came out in a husky growl. And the bitch actually smiled. "If you're looking for Trey, he just left. Oh, and he said he didn't want to mate with you." She shrugged and leaned against the doorframe. "Said something about winning a bet with his brothers."

Nichole's stomach burned with fear and a lump formed in her throat. No. April was lying. Trey had warned her. "I don't believe you."

Turning on her heels, Nichole headed to Trey's parent's house. She got a few feet down the path before April caught up with her. Pain sliced up Nichole's arm as the bitch gripped it in her claws. Nichole jerked around to face April. Fury boiled in her chest and she yanked her arm out of the bear's grasp, ignoring the sting of the other woman's nails tearing flesh.

"Trey is *my* mate. I feel him inside me."

April narrowed her eyes and streaks of gold rippled across her brown irises. "There will be no mating if I kill you and be there to help Trey pick up the pieces."

Enough. The bitch was crazy. There was no reasoning with crazy. Unfortunately, Nichole also knew she was no match for the bear.

"Trey!"

"Yell all you want. He can't hear you."

Nichole snapped her gaze to April's. Suspicion ran its icy fingers up her spine. "What did you do to him?"

"Something I should have done before now."

That was it. Nichole charged, throwing all her weight into the bear. April gasped for air and stumbled back, clearly not expecting the blow. Nichole took the chance to run back toward Trey's, but didn't get far before April grabbed a fist full of hair and jerked.

Nichole fell on her ass. Pain exploded in her hip and she cried out.

"What's wrong? Too fat to fight?"

Pushing away the pain, Nichole kicked out, catching April in the back of the knee. Instantly, the bear went down. A crack sounded as her head hit the ground, then her body went still.

Shit.

Nichole scrambled to the female's side. "April." No response. Heart pounding, Nichole shook her. Nothing. "Come on, April."

The bear's head fell to the side, sliding off a sharp rock coated in her blood. Nichole covered her mouth with her hands and scooted backwards. April couldn't be dead.

"Nichole?"

She jerked around to Anthony's voice. Her whole body shook and tears filled her eyes. "It was an accident. I—"

The Marshal glanced at April, then pulled out his cell and sent a text. Returning his phone to his pocket, he held out his free hand. "Where's Trey?"

Nichole took his hand. "I...I don't know."

Wait. April had been in his house. Her heart sank to her belly. What if she'd killed him? Releasing Anthony's hand, she darted up the porch steps and into the house. "Trey?"

She rushed through the living room to the hall and checked each bedroom. He wasn't there. When she checked the kitchen, fear rose from deep inside her. *No, no, no.* Trey lay on the floor, unmoving. She dropped to her knees and tapped his cheeks. "Please be alive."

Tears fell down her cheeks and she rested her head on his chest. The slow *thump* of his heart soothed her a little. After a few moments, he circled his arms around her and let out a soft growl.

"Why are you bleeding?"

She lifted her head and framed his face in her hands. "Are you okay?"

"Fine. Answer my question."

He was angry, but not at her. Somehow, she knew that. "April...We fought. I think I killed her."

His forehead creased as he raked his gaze over her and lifted her right arm to inspect the scratches. "Help me up, please."

She did as he asked. When he was to his feet, Anthony walked into the kitchen. "April will live. Unfortunately. That was her last chance. I'll arrange for her transfer back to the Rocky Mountains."

Trey nodded and rubbed the back of his head. "Bitch hit me with something."

Anthony glanced to Nichole and smiled. "I take it you're back to stay?"

She nodded and was pulled into a tight hug. "Welcome to the family."

"Thanks."

"You two take all the time you need to get the

newness out of your system. I have paperwork to do." Anthony rolled his eyes before he turned and left.

Trey stared at her, hope and happiness brightening his blue gaze. "You're here to stay?"

"Yes. Connie said I should stop thinking and 'get my ass mated.'"

He threw his head back and laughed, then picked her up and twirled her around. "I love you. I know you might think it's too soon, but it's not for me. I've loved you from the moment I saw you."

She sniffed and threw her arms around his neck. "I love you, too. I just didn't know it until I saw you on the floor and thought I'd lost you."

"It'll take more than a hit on the head to kill me." He peppered her face with kisses, then scooped her up in his arms.

When he began walking, she asked, "Where are we going?"

"To complete the mating. I want to feel you inside me mind, body, and soul for the rest of our lives."

"Sounds like a plan to me."

He burst into the master bedroom and laid her on the bed. His fingers caressed her forehead, then her cheek. "My beautiful mate. I'll love you always and forever."

"As will I. Now, make me yours, bear."
"Yes, ma'am."

The End

BEAR MAGICK

BEARS OF BLACKROCK, BOOK TWO

Bear Magick

Independent, curvy, and beautiful Connie Glover doesn't need a man in her life to make her happy. Or to save her. Or so she tells herself…

While out pursuing her passion for wildlife photography, she's confronted by a hunter with his sights set on dominating her. Determined to teach the human a lesson, she's a little annoyed when a sexy bear shifter shows up and chases the hunter away.

Anthony Black is the Marshal of Blackrock. His number one priority is protecting his den—and his mate. But keeping Connie safe is a challenge in itself. Not only is he unsure if she'll accept him, but the stubborn and sexy witch loves her independence. Almost as much as she loves teasing him—something that makes him mad with desire.

With new threats to the Pack rearing their ugly head, Anthony must find a way to win her heart while convincing her they're better together than apart. Because despite how hot her teasing makes him, securing her in his life and in his Pack is no laughing matter.

1

Connie crouched low behind some brush, careful to make as little sound as she could. Early evening in the Georgia Cohutta Wilderness was the perfect time to snap a few shots of the wildlife in the area. She breathed in the cool, fall mountain air and fought back a sigh. Fall was her favorite season. Time for pumpkins, spiced hot cider, cinnamon everything, and, best of all, colder weather.

Settling into her spot, she positioned the camera. A few yards away stood a family of deer: two fawns, a doe, and a buck. The buck, most likely the proud papa of the fawns, held his head up, watching for danger.

The perfect picture.

She removed the lens cap from her Nikon and

snapped a few shots. Papa deer rotated his head in her direction but didn't indicate he was about to run. *Good.* The setting sun bathed the mountainside in a hue of peach, adding to the perfection of the scene in front of her.

Her thrill of the moment faded as the hairs on the back of her neck stood on end and her skin tingled. *Crap.* She didn't need the bears snooping around. They always scared the wildlife away. Oh well, it was time to pack up her camera and head to Blackrock—the bear-shifter clan who lived in the area.

A few weeks before, her best friend had mated the youngest son of the Alpha. Connie couldn't be happier for Nichole. Trey treated her like a goddess, always pampering her. It was both great and sad at the same time. Well, the couple wasn't sad; Connie was. A little.

Seeing them so happily in love and planning their future had started her own biological clock. If only she could find a man who loved her—her snarkiness and her curves. Unfortunately, it appeared no such male existed. He'd love one or the other of those things, or none at all. Her last boyfriend had thought he could change her.

She snorted. Connie changed for no one.

She didn't need a man anyway. Besides, the wham-bam-don't-call-me-I'll-call-you worked for her. No strings attached. No broken heart.

After placing her camera in its bag, she stood and froze at a *schklikt* sounded from behind her. A gun being racked. Cold fear sliced into her chest. *Damn. Where's that bear when you need him?*

"Well, well. What do we have here?" A deep, husky voice brought her gaze up to the man's face. From his lack of a magickal aura, she could tell he was human. Although there was a darkness that surrounded him. She dismissed it as his character—a lonely, mean-ass man that got off on other's pain or misfortune.

"Just taking some pictures." She tried to keep her voice light and friendly as she hiked her bag higher on her shoulder and stepped past him.

The moment she was shoulder to shoulder with him, he grabbed her by the waist. She squeezed her eyes shut, not wanting to hurt the human. However, if he left her no choice, she'd defend herself. "Let me go."

"Oh, come on. How about a little fun."

Fun? Yeah, she'd have a little fun, turning him into the slimy slug he was. "I'm not going to ask again."

"Oh, I'm scared."

You should be. On the heels of her thought, the asshat grabbed her boob. That was it. She braced her feet, grabbed his arm, and threw him over her shoulder. His breath whooshed out as his back slammed against the ground.

Her temper flared, and she moved to stand in front of him, picking up the shotgun he'd dropped. She pointed the gun at him and narrowed her eyes. "I suggest you take your ass home and think twice before you try to assault another female."

The man's eyes grew round then he scrambled backward, got to his feet, and ran off.

She rolled her eyes, lowered the gun, and turned around. In his large black bear form, Anthony stared at her. With a sigh, she said, "The stupid human doesn't know that he shouldn't run from a bear."

A growled snort was his reply, but he didn't move.

"Are you going to stare at me all day? Ugh. Whatever." She bent to pick up her camera bag and checked the contents. A wave of relief fluttered through her when nothing appeared broken. She wouldn't really know until she got home and unpacked everything, however. Damn hunter.

When she turned to go to her car, parked about a ten-minute hike away, Anthony stepped in front of her. She crossed her arms and glared at him. "What?"

His black coat shimmered a moment before a flash of silver extended from him as he shifted into his human form, naked. *Good gods.* Broad shoulders, a chest ripped with hard muscles, trim waist, and... Well, the man was blessed in many ways.

"Are you going to stare at me all day?"

Touché. She held in her smile as she met his gaze. "I just might."

He worked his jaw then pivoted on his heels to walk away. After admiring his tight ass for a few moments, she followed him. One thing the hot-ass bear wasn't going to do was walk away from her. "What are you doing here?"

"I live here." He turned, and she had to jerk to a stop to keep from running into him. "Have you not noticed that you are in Blackrock?"

Of course, she'd noticed. She wasn't a dingbat. What did it a matter anyway? Her BFF was mated to Anthony's brother. That made Connie like a friend of the family, right? "Am I not welcome on bear territory?"

He narrowed his eyes, and the right corner of his

lips twitched. "I didn't say that... Anyway, as I said, I live here."

She chewed on her bottom lip to hide her smile. The sexy bear was flustered and growing erect. "I know where you live. In fact, I was on my way there before I saw a few deer. The lighting was perfect for a great shot so I stopped to try and capture the moment."

He glanced to her camera bag and grunted before turning to continue his trek into the woods. Smiling, she moved in step with him. "Even though I didn't need it, thank you for coming to my rescue."

Too fast for her to track, he twisted to face her and grabbed her wrist. Heat spread through her body, and damn if she didn't ache all over with need. The damn bear definitely awakened her libido.

He released a low growl. "I'm the Marshal of Blackrock. It's my *job* to protect the Pack."

She straightened her spine, which pushed her ample breasts into his bare chest, and lifted her brows. "When are you not working?"

He released her and stepped away. His blue eyes shimmered as he stared at her. "Never."

"Really? No downtime at all?" She stepped closer. A smile tugged at her lips when he didn't back away.

Suddenly, he closed the distance, wrapped an arm around her waist, and jerked her to him so their bodies were flattened together. "You like playing with bears?"

A growl rumbled from his chest, vibrating her to the soul. *This male is hot.* "I like playing with you."

"Careful what you ask for." Abruptly, he released her and pointed behind her. "I'll see you at the den." Then he shifted into the large, black bear once more and loped off in the direction of the Blackrock den.

Turning, she frowned at the sight of her old, faded red Beetle. If he thought to avoid her, he was mistaken. Anthony Black wasn't going to know what hit him. Whether he wanted to admit it or not, he was her mate.

~

ANTHONY BARRELED through his back door, which was the bear-size version of a dog door, and shifted to his human form. His blood still ran hot from the encounter with Connie. The memory of how the hunter had manhandled her sent a protective rage through him. No one touched her besides him.

Damn.

Fisting his hands, he marched to his bedroom to pull on a pair of jeans and a T-shirt. The damned female had cast a spell over him. Ever since they'd locked gazes at his brother's mating ceremony, Anthony hadn't been able to get the curvy, beautiful witch out of his mind. And his bear wanted to claim her—fast and hard.

The minx was headed to the den for dinner, most likely to spend time with his new sister-in-law, Nichole. As the Marshal, Anthony couldn't leave for the night. No, he had to suck it up and pray he had the strength to stay away from Connie.

Maybe he'd give a sentry the night off and take his post.

He entered the living room and picked up his cell as the front door opened. Lifting a brow at Trey, Anthony watched as the male came inside and dropped to the sofa. "Make yourself comfortable."

"I will." His brother grinned then propped his booted feet on the coffee table, crossing them at the ankles.

Anthony rolled his eyes and continued to the kitchen. "What do you want, Trey?"

Trey feigned shock. "I'm hurt. Do I need a reason to visit my brother?"

"Yes, especially since you are not here with your mate." After taking two beers out of the fridge, Anthony stepped into the living room and handed one of the longnecks to Trey.

"Nichole wants us to get the band together. She, Tiffany, and Mom are currently planning food for a cookout." Trey took a swig of his beer before meeting Anthony's glare. "I think it'll be fun."

Anthony growled low and tightened his grip on the bottle. So much for hiding out at a sentry post. Fuck. "Fine."

When Trey didn't move and continued to stare at him, dread cut through Anthony. His family had no doubt thought to play matchmakers. And Trey had drawn the short straw. "Just spit it out."

Trey shrugged. "Mom seems to think you and Connie would make a 'cute couple.' Her words."

Impossible. Leave it to his mother to scent out a mate for him. Or maybe she'd realized how Anthony's blood rushed in his veins whenever Connie was around. Either way, Mama Bear didn't give up once she had her mind made up.

He was doomed. There was no way he'd be able to keep his hands off the curvy goddess.

2

The beat of the music thumped through the air and on the ground, flowing around her. She swayed from side to side in tempo. Glee filled her as each note left the sensual mouth of the lead singer, Anthony.

His blue eyes met hers from time to time while he sang. Each glance sent a bolt of heat straight to her core. She let her gaze roam down his large, muscular body, loving the way his faded blue jeans hugged his form. A wave of heat washed over her, and she tore her gaze from him. Flashes of his naked body from earlier that evening filled her mind.

Damn. The urge to climb him, to lick every inch of him, grew stronger each time she saw him. Something about his stern glare, rugged unshaven face, and messy black hair stirred a primal need deep in her core. She couldn't sleep without him invading her dreams.

Oh gods, she had to get out of there before she did something crazy. Like jump him the first chance she got. Yet the three Black brothers, along with their dad, jammed out better than most pros she'd heard.

"Are you feeling well?" Nichole asked.

The bonfire lit up her face enough that Connie could see her friend's brows drawn together. Leaning her head on Nichole's shoulder, Connie let out a soft sigh. "I'm a little tired."

It wasn't a lie, but it wasn't the whole truth either. No, Connie would not be telling her BFF about her aching need to lick the dark-haired Marshal all over.

"Yeah. Me, too." Nichole rubbed her slightly swollen belly.

A wide smile lifted Connie's lips as her heart swelled. Nichole was two and a half months pregnant, which was equal to about four months for a normal human pregnancy. Shifter babies grew at a slightly faster rate.

Connie studied her friend for a few moments. A longing deep in her soul bloomed. Nichole radiated happiness and fairly glowed with her impending motherhood, something Connie wanted someday.

With a sigh, she glanced briefly to Anthony as he talked with his brothers. The thought of how overprotective Trey had been with Nichole *before* she got pregnant, then how he hovered even more now that she carried their cub filtered in. Connie wasn't sure she wanted someone hovering over her.

Bears, as well as other shifters, were like that. They protected their mates and family with their lives. And weren't afraid to show it.

The music stopped, and Connie took that time to make her escape. "I'd better be getting home before it gets any later."

Connie kissed her friend on the cheek and stood. After rising to her feet, Nichole drew her into a hug. "Stay the night."

"Thanks for the offer, but I have a few things to take care of in the morning." Connie tried to keep her tone calm, but she could tell that Nichole didn't buy the excuse. However, she didn't comment on it.

"Oh, okay. Drive careful."

Hugging her back, Connie almost caved in and agreed to Nichole's request. She couldn't do that. She couldn't stay that close to Anthony and actually get any sleep. "I'll text you when I get home."

Nichole's eyes brightened slightly. "Okay."

Connie turned, only to come face-to-face with

Anthony. The Marshal stared at her, his blue eyes boring into hers. "Leaving so soon?"

A lazy smile formed on her lips, and she closed the gap between them. "I have to work in the morning, but I could be persuaded to stay a little longer."

His eyes darkened as his body heat coiled around her, sending shivers of desire racing through her. "I thought we'd go for a walk."

Oh, man. This was a change from earlier that evening in the forest. Then again, he had warned her to be careful what she asked for. Blinking her eyes, she tried to give him a blank stare. "Why?"

"You know why," he growled.

Yeah, she knew. Tracing a finger up his cotton tee, she nibbled on her bottom lip. "I might."

He let out a frustrated breath, grabbed her wrist, and tugged her down a path leading to a small stream. She stifled a laugh as she stumbled forward to walk by his side. Wiggling her wrist out of his grasp, she linked their fingers. Anthony stiffened, making her smile a littler wider. "What do you plan to do with me?"

A low growl vibrated from him before he drew to a stop. His blues eyes narrowed, but his nostrils flared as if taking in her scent. After a moment, he leaned in so their lips were barely a breath apart. Her heart pounded in anticipation, the thought of finally tasting him making her lightheaded.

Suddenly, he released her and stepped back. His brows drew together, then his features hardened. "This can't happen. I have to go."

He took off deeper into the forest.

Stunned and confused at his change in mood, Connie just stood there, watching him disappear through the trees. What the hell just happened? She'd never read anyone wrong before. Her intuition had always been spot on. Apparently, she was wrong this time. Anthony wasn't her mate.

Tears blurred her vision as she pivoted around and rushed to her car, not bothering to get her purse from Nichole's house. Embarrassment over how she'd thrown herself at the bear over the last few weeks only made the tears fall faster.

Inside her Beetle, she took a deep breath. *You will not cry, damn it. No male is worth it, especially not Anthony Black.*

THE PAINFUL CRY of a cub sliced through Anthony's heart as he raced around trees, trying to reach the teen in record time. Thoughts of the hunter from earlier filled his mind. Other Packs around the area had said they'd seen an increase in activity. It didn't matter to most humans that it wasn't hunting season.

He slowed when he was within a few feet of the smaller bear. From his scent, Anthony knew it was sixteen-year-old Joseph, one of the junior soldiers. No other scent was in the area, telling him that the teen had come out here alone. But why?

Approaching the male, Anthony eased down beside him and carefully rested a hand on his shoulder. The boy cried out. That was when Anthony saw the bear trap around Joseph's foot.

Fuck. "Easy, Joe. Trey is on his way to help me with this." Anthony had sensed his brother a few moments before finding the teen.

Just then, Trey broke through the trees and let out a string of curses. "Fucking hunters."

Anthony agreed. "This is way too personal now. The bastards need to be stopped."

Trey nodded and proceeded to pry the trap open. Anthony gently slid Joseph's foot out of it then picked him up. Holding him in a tight hug, Anthony raced back to the Medical Center at the center of the den. The kid would mend with the help of their Healer.

When he reached the den, Anthony frowned at the empty parking spot where Connie's car had sat earlier. Dread hit him like a weight as he realized he'd left her at the stream without any explanation.

And then the words he'd uttered came back to him, haunting him. *This can't happen. I have to go.*

Good one, asshole.

At the time, Anthony's only concern was getting to Joseph. It hadn't occurred to him what he sounded like. An ass rejecting his mate.

3

"We found about a dozen traps set within a twenty-mile radius of the den."

Anthony ground his teeth at the snarled out statement from one of his senior enforcers, Ian. A dozen traps was not just one or two hunters. No, it sounded like a group of poachers. "Have you reached out to the park rangers?"

"This morning. They said they ran off a couple of hunters a few days ago and have been keeping an eye out." Ian stood and moved toward the door. "I'll put a few more sentries out and let the females know to keep the children inside the den."

The children were the number one priority. Anthony hated to limit them to the den, but he couldn't take the chance of anyone else getting hurt or possibly killed. "Good. We all need to do our part to keep the den safe."

Ian gave a short nod and left the office. Alone, Anthony's thoughts returned to Connie. She hadn't returned his messages, or answered her phone any of the times he'd called. He fisted his hand briefly before picking up his cell and dialing his sister-in-law.

"Hello."

"Hi, Nichole. Have you talked to Connie this morning?"

"Yeah, I just got off the phone with her." There was a slight hint of sadness in the female's voice that sparked his bear's interest.

"What's wrong?"

Nichole fell silent for a few moments. When she finally spoke, there was annoyance in her tone, as well. "What did you say to her last night?'

Fuck. Releasing a heavy sigh, he leaned back in his leather chair and ran a hand through his hair. "I took her to the stream to talk without the family listening in. Before I got a chance to... I heard Joe's cry in the distance. God, I'm an idiot."

Nichole made a growl-like sound. "She's pretty upset. And embarrassed. You may have to grovel. A lot. But it'll have to wait. She's visiting her aunt at

Ashwood today. You can catch her at the photo shop tomorrow. That way, she can't run from you."

The photo shop, formally known as Con's Little Shop of Memories, was Connie's one-hour photo store. Nichole said she'd opened it in college for extra pocket change, not knowing how successful it would become.

Waiting until the next day to corner her at her job would drive him mad. He could call the Alphas of Ashwood and get clearance to visit. But on what grounds? That he wanted to charge in and drag his mate home? Yeah, that would go over well. But there was an alternative. He could wait for her at her house with dinner for when she returned home. "Any suggestions on how to grovel? And would you be willing to help me out?"

Nichole laughed. "Chocolate is always good. Her favorite sweet treat is chocolate covered strawberries. And yeah, come over later."

Those few words helped ease his bear a little. It was still going to be a long day and night. "Thanks, Nichole."

"No need to thank me. The hard part is all up to you." She paused, and he heard Trey's voice in the background. A moment later, Nichole said, "I'll talk to you later."

"Okay, later." He ended the call.

Rising, he sent his enforcers a text to meet him where he'd found Joe the night before. They were going to set their own little traps for the humans and let them know to stay off their land.

~

"He's so precious." Connie's heart swelled as she looked into the angelic face of her newest cousin. Wesley was adorable and perfect in every way.

"Thank you," both his mom, Shayna Hunter, and his grandmother—Robyn Hunter, Connie's aunt—said at the same time.

Connie smiled, even though her pride was still hurt over a certain bear that had haunted her dreams the night before. Pushing away the depressing thoughts, she glanced up at her aunt. Robyn frowned.

"What is it?"

Shrugging, Connie averted her gaze to watch the sleeping baby. "I made a fool of myself over a male. It's over now, so I'd like to talk about something else."

Robyn shook her head. "You know me better

than that. I'm sure whatever you did will pass. Besides, it can't be worse than anything I've done."

Always look to the positive. Those were Robyn's words. She'd lived by them, and had spoken them to Connie for as long as she could remember. They usually made Connie feel better. Not this time. "Did you throw yourself at a male only to get rejected?"

"Yep. It was when I meet Travis's father. I was young and a little wild for the time period. When I first saw him, I knew he had to be my mate. I followed him around and tried many times to seduce him." Robyn paused, and a smile formed on her face as if the memories were among the happiest of those she kept close to her heart.

"What happened?" Shayna asked.

Robyn glanced from the beautiful blonde back to Connie. "One evening, I thought I'd finally gotten him to admit we were mating. He agreed to meet me for dinner. He never showed. When I called him, he didn't answer. I was crushed."

A lump lodged in Connie's throat. She knew too well what that rejection felt like. Before she could ask her aunt to continue, Robyn spoke. "I avoided him for days until he cornered me at the market. He explained that his father had gotten shot while on a hunt. I felt awful for thinking the worst."

Oh no, that would be awful...

The night before flashed in Connie's mind... Anthony's desire-filled gaze staring into hers. His bear so close to the surface she could feel the beast with her empathy. Then something she hadn't noticed at the time came to her. The quick flash of fear followed by anger and protectiveness that had clouded his blue eyes right before he muttered his statements and ran off.

Oh, gods, she was an awful, whiny bitch.

"Connie, are you all right?"

"No. I jumped to a conclusion without searching out the truth." Connie dropped her shoulders and laid back against the couch.

"He'll forgive you." Shayna's statement drew Connie's attention.

"I'm not sure I can face him now."

Robyn reached over and covered her hand. "Honey, go home and call him. Hear him out."

"What if I'm wrong again?"

"What if you were never wrong?"

Connie frowned. The hopeful part of her wanted to run out the door and go to Anthony. Another part of her wanted to give him a little longer. Gods, she'd never been so confused in her life. "I'll call him tonight."

Tightening her grip on Connie's hand, Robyn stood and tugged her to a stand. "Oh, no. You're not putting it off. You and I can spend time together anytime."

Connie opened her mouth to argue, but closed it. There was no arguing with her aunt, so she allowed Robyn to walk her to her vehicle. With a forced smile, Connie said her goodbyes and started her car.

She was about halfway through her hour-long drive home when a car came up behind her, too fast. Her heart raced, and she turned her wheel to the right to avoid being hit from behind. The car jerked at the last minute but not fast enough. It clipped the bumper of her Beetle, sending it swirling across the road and onto the left shoulder. She stopped inches from the rock face of the mountain.

Fucking idiot. She closed her eyes and took deep, calming breaths. Her pulse raced so fast she felt it throughout her body. Her hands tingled with her magick—ready to protect herself in an instant.

A moment later, her car door jerked open. She screamed and flung up her hands, an iridescent wall of power going up around her.

"Connie."

That voice. She glanced up into the face of Anthony. Her vision blurred slightly. Pulling back her magick, she dissolved the protective wall and flung herself at him.

"Shh." He hugged her tightly and kissed her head. "You're safe."

Yes, she was safe. With Anthony, always. Why didn't he see it? She pushed out of his hold and glanced around. The car that had run her off the road was nowhere to be seen. Annoyed at whoever the asshat was—and for her own weakness—she focused back on Anthony, her eyes narrowing. "I'm still mad at you."

Instead of replying, he lifted her into his arms, carried her to the other side of the car, and eased her into the seat. She waited until he'd wrapped the blanket from the back seat around his waist to cover himself and climbed in the driver's side before asking, "What are you doing?"

"I'm taking you home and making you dinner," he said as he pulled onto the road.

Taking her home and making her dinner? She was only run off the road. She wasn't injured, and she sure as hell wasn't helpless. Studying his profile, she asked, "What's with the sudden interest in me?"

A low growl of irritation rumbled inside the car. "It's not sudden."

"Could have fooled me." She muttered the words

as she peered out the window to watch the trees blur by. The Bug seemed to grow smaller with Anthony in it. It was also strange to ride in the passenger seat of her own car. However, she was grateful that the bear had shown up.

The feeling of belonging returned like it always did while in his presence. One way or another, she needed to know if he felt the pull. Only then could she move on with her lonely life.

4

Anthony hated that Connie still shook from the accident. She tried to hide it, but he saw the way her hands timbered slightly as she unlocked the door to her house. Her scent, however, had soured to anger.

He followed her inside, bracing himself for her reaction when she realized that he'd already been there. Nichole had given him the spare key to Connie's home so he could surprise the female when she got back from her aunt's place.

Even though, according to Nichole, it was too early to grovel for Connie's forgiveness, he'd felt that something wasn't right, and had opened his senses to Connie. A hint of worry mixed with distress had touched his awareness.

Although rare with mates, he'd instantly

connected to Connie the moment they met. His bear was hypersensitive to her and knew when she needed him or was about to tease him in that way she always did.

"You've been in my house."

He met her annoyed, accusing glare and smiled. "Nichole gave me her key. I was going to surprise you."

Folding her arms, she sharpened her stare. "How did you know I was run off the road?"

"I didn't until I got to you. I just felt that something was wrong, shifted, and ran out to find you." He moved past her, not sure how to tell her about the mating urge, or the link his bear had already formed. Sure, he knew she was attracted to him. She'd made attempts to keep her feelings from him. But mating was different. It was for a lifetime.

The female had to accept it wholeheartedly or they'd never share the full bond with each other.

Glancing at her over his shoulder, he asked, "Why did you leave last night?"

She pushed by him, entered the kitchen, and started going through the reusable bags he'd left on the counter before he rushed out to track her. He rushed to her side and grabbed her hands before she found the strawberries. "Answer the question."

Dropping her shoulders, she spoke softly. "You left me by the stream, said 'This can't happen,' and ran off."

The hurt that flashed in hers eyes before she looked away stabbed him in the heart. Damn, he was an ass. He drew her into him and wrapped his arms around her. "One of the junior soldiers got caught in a trap. I didn't think about what I said, I just reacted. My only thought was getting to the teen."

She hugged him back then. "I'm sorry."

"Don't be. I was an ass. I should have told you what was going on and sent you back to the den." He pulled back and framed her face. "This dinner is me groveling."

She glanced at the bags. "What are we having?"

"Chicken penne Alfredo with garlic knots."

Her face lit up. "And dessert? I smell chocolate."

He turned her around and walked her out of the kitchen. "That is a surprise. Go relax while I cook."

A slight smile formed on her lips when she glanced at him before disappearing into what he assumed was her bedroom.

∽

Connie stepped out of the shower to the wonderful aromas of pasta, cheese sauce, garlic, and bread. She had no idea what the bear was up to, but she wasn't going to argue with anyone who would make a meal for her. Apparently, by the smells swirling in her house at the moment, the male could cook.

After dressing, she made her way through the living room to the dining area adjacent to the kitchen. Anthony was now dressed and bent over, pulling the garlic knots out of the oven. Without turning to her, he said, "Have a seat."

She thought about being defiant, but her stomach growled, telling her she'd better obey. She'd been so upset over the situation with him the night before that she hadn't eaten breakfast and only half of her lunch.

"You shouldn't skip meals." Anthony ignored her sharp glare and set their plates on the table before retrieving the bread. One of the first things he'd noted when he reached her on the road, besides her fear, was her hunger. Her stomach had rumbled and her scent was slightly sweeter than normal.

When he came back, he sat next to her and smiled as she inhaled and almost groaned at the combinations of smells. "Oh, trust me, I don't usually. After all, I have to keep my girly figure up."

Running a hand over her curvy hips, she sent him a half smile. She'd never had issues with being a full-figured woman. In fact, she'd learned growing up to love who she was—curves and all. Those that were bothered by it could go to hell for all she cared. All that mattered was that she was secure and happy with herself.

Anthony leaned into her and nipped at her nose. "I love your *womanly* figure."

A jolt of desire raced through her veins. She could eat him up. Maybe she'd have *him* for dessert. "Good."

He scooped a forkful of pasta and offered it to her. Taking a bite, she closed her eyes. The cheesy, creamy sauce was perfect, and the pasta was just right. Not too firm, not too soft. "This is good. Did you really make this?"

"I'm hurt." He stuck his bottom lip out, but she could see the smile he tried to hide. "Yes, I made it. From scratch."

"Well, then, you need to come over and cook for me every day."

"I'd love to, if you'll move in with me."

She gasped, which made her cough a few times before she stared at him. "What?"

His eyes lit up with laughter as he reached for her hands. When she allowed him to take them, his features relaxed. "I've known for a while that you are my mate. I just didn't know how you would react. I mean, I know you like me, but do you understand what it means to mate a bear?"

Tightening her grip on his hands, she smiled. "My aunt is half wolf and was mated to a wolf. Am I correct to assume it's similar?"

"It is, in that we mate for life and our souls bond." He paused and brought her knuckles to his lips. "I was also afraid you wouldn't feel the mating urge."

He was too cute. The big, strong bear Marshal was worried about mating. "I know you are my mate. For witches, it's knowing that someone is magickally compatible, if that makes sense."

"Is it like the bear knowing by scent and taste?"

"Yeah, I guess it is. Witches see auras, and their mate is revealed to them with that energy." She took a bite of her food and watched him process what she'd said.

His lips twitched as he glanced from her face to her plate. "You know I'm going to claim you tonight."

She shrugged and tried to stop the desires burning inside of her from taking over. "I had my hunches."

He let out a low growl that sent a shudder of desire through her. Her mouth watered and her hands itched to touch him. She didn't need her magick to know what the bear had in mind. She could tell by the hungry gleam in his eyes.

"Do you accept the mating?"

She held up a hand. "Not so fast, furball. Don't put words in my mouth. I just said I know how this mating dance thing works. But I also know we don't fully bond until I give my heart to you completely."

He stared at her, one brow raised. "Furball?"

"Is that all you heard me say?"

A lazy, sexy smile formed on his sensual lips. "I heard everything you said, female." He gripped the chair arms and pulled her, chair and all, closer to him. "My plan is to pleasure you until you don't have a choice but to complete the bond."

"Until I have no choice?" It was her turn to raise a brow.

He twined his fingers into the hair at her nape and tugged, exposing her neck to him. A shot of excitement raced through her, hot and cold at the same time. She almost came at the growl in his voice when he whispered, "Let me rephrase. You won't want to choose anything else but a lifetime bound to me."

Oh, good gods. The male was definitely not used to being denied. Although, she wasn't denying him. The mating urge was too strong within her, yet she wasn't sure if she was ready. Sure she chased him and teased him, but the reality of a lifetime commitment gave her pause. She'd lived too long as an independent female, playing by her rules only. She didn't want that to change.

"I need a little time. I'm as stubborn as you are, and not used to being bossed around or sharing my life or soul with anyone besides Nichole." She frowned at her own words. "That sounded selfish."

He cupped her face, his thumb running over her bottom lip. "The first year, or maybe longer, is always about finding the balance. The good thing about it, is that there will be plenty of make-up sex."

He was good at the sweet talk. "I still need to get it straight in my head first."

He captured her lips in a bone-melting, toe-curling kiss. Opening to him, she groaned as tingles skittered over her flesh and desire pooled between her thighs. When he broke the kiss, she reached for him, only to have him grip her wrist. "Don't think that I'm going to leave and let you think about it."

"It's a good thing I'm great at multitasking."

He chuckled and yanked her shirt over her head. Lifting his head, he licked his lips as if he wanted to devour her. She was going to let him. If that kiss were any indication of the kind of pleasure he could bring her, she would be stupid to walk away from him.

The moment his lips touched her skin, she grew wetter and her skin heated. He slid his hand down her side to the waist of her jeans. With a quick jerk, he ripped her jeans from her. "You're lucky those weren't my favorite pair."

"Am I?"

"Yes. I'd have to punish you if they were."

Releasing a claw, he sliced through her bra and tugged it off her, then discarded the thing on the floor. He nipped at her breast just above her nipple. She sucked in a breath as he slid his lips over the tight bud and took it between his teeth. Pleasure bloomed inside her. Her whole body was on fire, and her patience thinned with each lick and caress.

He abandoned her breast and trailed feather-like kisses down her stomach and farther. Brushing her panties to the side, he licked her clit. She cried out and moved her hips in time with his mouth. Desire ran rapid in her blood, making her flesh all the more sensitive to him.

Good gods, if this were anything like what it would be like to mate with the bear, then sign her up. His gentle caresses and commanding touches sent her into a blissful state she never wanted to come down from.

His mouth covered her pussy, sucking, while he inserted two fingers inside. She fisted her hands in his hair and lifted her hips off the couch. Dizzying passion swirled in her head, and a drunken need overrode her thoughts. He pumped his fingers in and out, faster and harder. Pressure built until her body convulsed and an orgasm shattered through her.

Panting, she rode the last of the climax and heard his zipper lower. A moment later, he filled her, stretching her completely. Much too sensitive, she cried out in pleasure again and gripped his arms. His thrusts drove her over the edge over and over. How many times? Hell if she knew.

His body tensed right before he roared out his own climax. He eased out, then back in and shuddered over her. Cupping his face in her hands, she kissed him. He was beautiful when he came.

She smiled at him. "I think I need more convincing."

A lazy half smile formed on his face. "You are a naughty witch."

"I never said I was good."

He kissed her forehead and pulled out completely. "I want to take you in every room in this house, then in mine."

Well, hell, she wouldn't be able to walk. She might not even be able to talk after all that. But like he'd said, she was a naughty witch. "Which room is next?"

"I'm thinking the bathroom, then the bedroom." He lifted her in his arms and carried her toward the shower.

What had she gotten herself into? A lifetime of bliss and happiness it seemed. But she didn't let him know her decision was made, not yet.

5

Thoughts of Anthony whirled in her mind all day. She didn't remember the last time she'd smiled so much or ached in all the right places. The male was sensual, compassionate, and pure alpha male. Everything she loved and wanted in a mate.

Loved.

Yeah, she was falling for him. Even after spending just one night with him, she knew it wouldn't be long before she caved. Hell, she'd known after the first time they made love. The next few times were her undoing. She would open up to him and accept the man and the bear as hers.

She was about to be a mated female. There was no holding back her feelings after the night she'd had.

Goodbye single life.

The bell on the door dinged, and Connie cringed. It never failed that a customer would come in ten minutes before closing. Well, whoever it was would have to wait until the next day to get their photos back. Unless they were picking up an order. Connie had already shut down the machine. Sure, it could be restarted, but she had a hot date. Literally.

"How can I help you?" She glanced up at the customer and froze. Fury rose up, and she fisted her hands as she watched the man.

His bushy eyebrows were drawn together and looked like a large, black, fuzzy worm across his forehead. Opening her senses, she called her to her magick and focused on his body language as well as his emotions, which flowed around him like angry bees. The man had issues, and she guessed it had nothing to do with her. His aura was darker than it had been the other day in the forest. Odd.

"I was passing by and thought I'd stop by and say hi."

Bullshit. He was lying. His lack of eye contact, as well as her intuition told her that. Her first guess was that he'd followed her.

She squared her shoulders and lifted her chin. Deciding to play dumb and act like she didn't recognize him, she narrowed her eyes slightly, studying him as if seeing him for the first time. "Have we met?"

He slammed his hands on the counter, making her jump. "Two days ago up the mountain. I believe you threatened me with my own shotgun."

Yeah, she remembered. She'd tried to keep the human from getting hurt. She couldn't kill him, but she could make him wish he were dead. Then there was Anthony. She closed her eyes at the thought. No, she needed to deal with the human herself.

"Look, you were acting like an ass, and I did what I had to in order to protect you and myself."

He threw his head back and laughed. "The only reason I didn't teach you a lesson was because of that huge-ass bear." He narrowed his eyes. "How did you escape the beast?"

She grinned while spreading her fingers to allow building power to spread to her fingertips. "Just call me the bear whisperer."

His eyes narrowed as he studied her. A knowing brushed against her subconscious. He tsked and moved closer. "You don't fear me?"

It was her turn to laugh. The cocky SOB didn't know the half of it. She was scared, terrified that the bastard would kill her or worse, go after the bears. And those bears were her family now. No one messed with her family. But she wouldn't let him know that.

"I don't fear pigheaded bastards like you."

One, two... With speed too fast for the human to track, she gripped his forearm as he swung at her and pushed her magick into him. Then she directed it to his chest to mimic a heart attack. He gasped and jerked his arm, trying to break her hold.

She leaned over the counter and spoke in a low growl-like tone, "I can end your life before you can blink. Now, I'm only going to say this once because I hate repeating myself. You will not come back here. In fact, I want you to move at least five states away and never come back."

The brown in his eyes darkened as he stared back at her. Dread crept over her. The persuasion spell didn't work. Why wouldn't it work?

"Your spells don't work on me, witch."

Suddenly, his features shifted into a demonic wolf. Cold fear froze her in place. *Mutant*. But how? Mutants were dumb, blood-crazed monsters. And they didn't have the ability to hide their scent. Then what was he?

The front door flew open. Anthony's earthy scent filled the room. A moment later, the hunter was yanked away from the counter. It took Connie a few moments to focus on what was happening.

Anthony punched the hunter, knocking him back several steps. The man...creature, charged Anthony like a linebacker. The two males crashed through the large window of her store and onto the sidewalk.

Connie's heart sank, and she wanted to scream from the mounting frustration. Running outside, she threw her hands up, raising a circle around the battling males to keep the humans from seeing what was going on. No need to let the humans know there were shifters, witches, and other magickal creatures in their world.

Helplessness chocked her, raising a panic she'd never felt before. She couldn't get a good shot at the hunter, so blasting the bastard with a spell was out because she'd never forgive herself if she accidently hurt Anthony.

A crack of bone echoed around her. She snapped her gaze to the males, her focus on Anthony. Something flashed in the hunter's hand a moment before he slammed it into Anthony's side. He staggered back a few steps, then charged at the other male. What the hell had the hunter hit her mate with? She let out a human growl then whirled around at the sound of footfalls behind her.

Trey and Ryan marched toward her. Relief rippled through her at the sight of Anthony's brothers. She faced them fully and pointed to Anthony and the hunter. "Please tell me that is not a mutant."

Ryan growled. "It's not a mutant." Without another word, he shifted into a large black bear and barreled over to the fighting males.

Trey held her gaze, a mixture of worry and anger swirling in the depths. "I need you to go to the den."

"No. I can't leave him." She glanced to Anthony and winced as he was kicked off the hunter and slid across the pavement. "Plus, when I leave, the circle keeping the humans from seeing everything will fall."

"Don't worry about that. Ryan can take care of it."

"What?"

Trey fisted his hands. "Please, Connie. I need you to keep Nichole from following me here. I can't worry about my pregnant mate and take care of shit here at the same time."

Confused, Connie glanced at Anthony and noticed that he'd begun to slow down. "What's happening to him?"

"My guess is that he was poisoned, but I won't know for sure until we stop that demon."

Connie began to shake. When she took a step toward the males, Trey gripped her upper arms. "Please, Connie, go to Nichole. I'm dead twice if anything happens to the both of you."

She sharpened her gaze on his and snarled. "You bring my mate home alive."

"I plan to."

She hesitated a moment before rushing to her car. Her heart broke with each mile she put between her and Anthony. Trey and Ryan would take care of him, or she'd kill both of them.

～

Anthony's vision blurred in and out. He shook his head, trying to clear the haze of the poison the demon had injected him with. Staggering forward, he swung and managed to somehow connect with the bastard's chin. The hit wasn't as effective as it should have been.

The demon charged at him, hitting him in the gut with his shoulder. Anthony fought to breathe as he stumbled back a few feet. *Damn it*. He had to clear his system. But how? He didn't have anything on him. No salt, and the connection to his mate had dulled to almost nothing.

Someone grabbed him by the waist from behind. He swung again, missing his target. Then he scented his brothers, and Ryan shouted, "Get him home. Now. I got this."

Anthony shook his head and tried to break out of Trey's hold. "No. We fight together. I'm the Marshal, damn you. Let me go."

"Not in this condition," Trey mumbled as he heaved Anthony over his shoulder. "You know as well as I do that demon can't kill Ryan. No matter what he does."

Anthony nodded, not caring that Trey couldn't see him do so. The world started to spin, and Anthony thought he was going to be sick. "Connie," he breathed.

"Safe at home."

Good. He squeezed his eyes shut, fought a wave of nausea, and welcomed the darkness.

6

Connie paced the living room of her best friend's home. Anthony's mom, dad, and sister were there, each one as worried as she was. Everything from the time the hunter—demon—had walked into her shop replayed over and over in her mind. "I don't understand how I never picked up on the fact that he was a demon. I should have been able to see it in his aura. I studied them for years with my coven."

"There are some demons that can go undetected by all magick-born, including shifters. I've run across a few of them. They disguise their sent and even their energy so they smell and look fully human." Elijah—her future father-in-law and the bear Alpha—spoke with a calm that made Connie want to scream.

She knew he was right, but she didn't want to believe that she was vulnerable to creatures like the hunter. "He could have killed me in the woods the other day."

"That's what worries me. He tracked you down. It makes me wonder who he was after," Elijah wondered aloud. Connie noted the frown on his face as he too began to pace.

She stopped next to Nichole and placed a hand on her shoulder. Tiffany sat next to her and held her hand. "Trey said Ryan could take care of the humans if they saw anything. What did he mean?"

It was Madison who answered. "Ryan has abilities."

Tiffany let out a sob as Elijah let out a low growl. "What I'm about to tell you is family business. You will not repeat it to anyone, ever."

Cold dread sliced through Connie. She glanced to the other females before meeting the Alpha's stare. "I give you my word as Anthony's mate."

"Ryan was marked by a demon about six years ago." Elijah glanced to Tiffany briefly before continuing. "The demon kidnapped Tiffany while she and Ryan were on one of their hunts. Tiffany was fourteen and had just shifted for the first time a few months before, so Ryan took her out to hunt for the first time. I heard Ryan's roar and felt his pain in my heart. By the time the boys and I got to him, he had already tracked down the demon. And made his bargain for her release."

Oh, no. He didn't. "What kind of deal?"

Elijah fisted his hands. "He refuses to tell me."

She guessed she didn't need to tell the Alpha that a deal with a demon meant giving up one's freedom, or even life.

The front door flew open and Trey entered with an unconscious Anthony over his shoulder. Connie rushed after Trey as he carried her mate to the guest room and laid him on the bed. A moment later, the Pack Healer, Holt Connor, rushed in. He ripped Anthony's shirt off and placed his hands on the Marshal's chest. Then he leaned in and inhaled.

Connie had never watched a shifter Healer work before, but she knew when to keep her mouth shut. Glancing at her, Holt softened his expression. "Pull that chair over and hold his hand. It will keep him calm while I work. He's worried about you."

Nodding, she did as she was told. A soon as their hands connected, she released a heavy sigh. A single tear rolled from her eye and her nose tingled. It was great to feel his energy and warmth. Dipping her head, she kissed his forehead. "I'm here, my mate."

Holt jerked back with his hands in the air. "Sorry. I wasn't expecting that."

"What?" Connie asked, alarm making her voice a few levels higher.

"The mating bond." Holt relaxed and urged her on. "Complete the bond. Open your heart to him and make your vow to be his forever."

"How will that help? He's been poisoned."

"It will speed up the healing process. I can focus on removing the poison while you heal the rest of him."

She focused on Anthony's pale features and didn't need to be a Healer to know he didn't have much time left. Squeezing his hand tighter and drawing it to her heart, she spoke her vows. "I am yours for as long as we both shall live. I promise to love and protect you with all of my power." She kissed his lips, quick. "You are mine, furball, and I'm not going to let you go."

By one slow thread after another she felt the mating weave into place. Their souls touched, and she inhaled a sharp breath when the bond completed with a snap, and a power she'd never known existed flowed through her. His strength mingled with her magick in a brilliant twine of energy. It felt amazing. On instinct, she pushed that power into Anthony, knowing he needed it more than she did.

A wave of dizziness crashed over her. Someone called her name, but she was too zoned in on healing her mate. Yet, she was so tired. Her eyes shut and she felt arms lift her. Then a soft male voice that sounded a lot like Elijah said, "Sleep my child. Everything will be clearer in the morning."

She nodded and submitted to sleep, knowing her mate was near and would be okay.

∾

ANTHONY WOKE with the realization that he was fully mated to the female curled up next to him. She'd saved his life. Well, with the help of his brothers and Holt. Although everything was fuzzy, he remembered almost everything that had happened. Especially the mating bond snapping into place.

She stretched and sighed softly. When her eyes fluttered open, he smiled at her. "Morning, beautiful."

Sitting up, she framed his face. "How do you feel? Do you need anything?"

"The only thing I need is your naked, curvy body against mine."

She laughed. "That can be arranged."

"There's only one problem, though." He nipped her nose.

"What?"

"My family is waiting for us to wake up."

She sighed. "Yes. I sensed them, too. I guessed they would wait a few more hours. I know a spell that could soundproof the room."

His dick jerked to attention. "I like the way you think."

She chanted something in Latin then straddled him. He grinned like an idiot when he noticed she was already bare to him. When she took him in her hand and guided his cock to her entrance, he jerked his hips up, thrusting into her.

Cupping her face, he brought her down until their lips touched. "I love you. I've loved you from the moment I saw you."

"I love you, too."

Flipping them over, he pushed inside her deeper. She groaned and scored his back with her nails. "I'll protect you always. You are mine as I am yours."

She groaned again and wrapped her legs around him. "Yes. Always."

Her pleasure hit him hard, building with his own. He increased his rhythm until an orgasm slammed into the both of them.

Lying beside her, he tucked her into his side and kissed her temple. "After we meet with my family, I'm taking you home. We won't leave that house for weeks."

"Weeks? I'm thinking months."

He laughed. "I love you, female."

"Love you too, furball."

"Let's go before they send someone in after us." Frowning, he added, "Has Ryan come by?"

Her worry hit him like a wave crashing over him. "I don't know. I've been with you since Trey brought you here."

He kissed her forehead. "He's alive. That much I know, but he's blocking us through the family bond." Rising from the bed, he gripped the chair next to the bed and waited for the sudden dizziness to go away before he dressed.

Connie scooted out of bed, gathered her clothes, and darted into the bathroom. Before she closed the door, she glanced over her shoulder at him. "Go be with your family and check on Ryan. I'm going to clean up. Unless you need me to go with you."

"Take your shower and meet us in the living

room. One thing about my family, you never get much privacy." He sent her a wink, but he was serious. His brothers and Tiffany didn't know the meaning of knocking before entering each other's home. It was something he'd grown up accepting. Connie may have a hard time with it, though, so he'd have to keep the doors locked.

Connie smiled then rushed to his side. She stood on her toes and kissed him. "Thanks for the warning. I'll manage. Plus, I like your family."

His chest tightened. Gods he loved that female. He swatted her on the ass, drawing a squeak from her. "Go shower."

Leaving Connie, even to walk the few feet to the living room, was the hardest thing he'd done in his life. He'd been serious when he told her he wanted to lock them in his house and not come out for weeks.

Anthony met his father's gaze as he entered the living room. His features were etched with anger and worry. "How bad is Ryan?"

The Alpha shook his head. "He killed the demon. Or at least had help killing the creature, which gave him another notch in that damn demon mark he carries. Although your stubborn-ass brother won't talk about it."

With a heavy heart, Anthony sat on the sofa next to Tiffany. "He's alive. That's all that matters now."

Nichole cleared her throat and spoke softly. "Connie studied demonology with her aunt and a few other witches when she was younger. We can see if she knows how to remove the mark."

"I'll ask her," Anthony said with a little more hope than before.

Tiffany jumped to her feet. Her feeling of discomfort heavy in her scent. "I have a great idea that will add some cheer to all you gloomy people. Let's have Ant and Connie's mating ceremony on Winter Solstice. I'll handle all the food and manage the decorations. It'll be fun and magickal!"

Smiling, Anthony rose and hugged his sister. "That will be great. The den deserves to celebrate."

Ryan would be okay. He had to be. The whole bear clan would fight to make sure of it. As for Anthony, he'd protect his brother, family, and his new mate.

New mate. Love filled his heart. He was about to share his life with Connie. He'd have it no other way.

The End

A BEARY SWEET HOLIDAY

BEARS OF BLACKROCK, BOOK THREE

A Beary Sweet Holiday

The kitchen isn't the only thing heating up this winter...

Tiffany Black, culinary artist and owner of Beary Sweets Café, is determined to make this year's Winter Solstice celebration one to remember. Especially since it will also be the mating ceremony for her brother, Anthony, and soon-to-be sister-in-law, Connie. She wants everything to be perfect. Unfortunately, you can't always get what you want. When she falls off a ladder in her café and breaks her ankle, she fears her plans are doomed. Until the sexy bear Healer, Holt, comes to the rescue—stirring up more than just recipes.

Mating has never been at the top of Holt's to-do list, and he's known Tiffany all her life. So when the mating urge slams into him after mending her ankle, he's taken aback—unsure and intrigued at the same time. The girl he watched grow up is now a curvy, sensual woman, and his bear wants to claim her. He wants to claim her.

The stubborn female refuses to follow Healer's

orders and allow her ankle to heal, and she's hell-bent on catering the winter celebrations. In order to do what needs to be done, she insists that he help her. Since it gives him an excuse to stay by her side, he's all right with that. As they work side by side to make the Solstice unforgettable, their passions ignite, and things turn utterly delicious.

1

A *freaking snow storm.*

Tiffany grumbled to herself as she packed up ingredients, kitchen tools she didn't have at home, and a few small appliances. If she were going to be stuck inside the Blackrock den for the gods knew how long, she needed her mobile kitchen. At least the things she didn't keep on hand at home.

The forecast called for a storm to move in overnight and dump a shit-ton of snow on the area. Since she was planning and catering the Winter Solstice/Anthony and Connie's mating ceremony and didn't want to be stuck at her café in Blue Ridge, Georgia, she had to pack up and work from her home.

Safe and warm.

The celebration was a little more than thirty-six

hours away. The beautiful, four-layer masterpiece of a cake was almost complete. She'd worked on it for the last two days, getting the frosting as smooth as she could and ready to decorate with the small bear-molded fondant and other special touches she would add the morning of the party.

Folding the flaps on the box to temporarily seal it, she scanned the small café with a sigh. She'd opened Beary Sweets about two years ago thanks to the support of her family. They'd encouraged her to pursue her love of food and baking and turn it into a career. She didn't regret a thing. She loved her restaurant.

"I think this is the last of it," Kaylee, her employee and one of her best friends, said as she set a box on the counter next to Tiffany's.

Tiffany nodded. "All but the cake." Just then, her brother Ryan entered, the chime on the door *dinging* as it opened.

Tiffany smiled. Ryan was the middle brother and her favorite—if she had to pick one. All of her brothers were different versions of their father with black hair and blue eyes, each one slightly just as protective in their own way.

Anthony was the one who'd insisted on the high-tech security system in Beary Sweets. As the born

Marshal, he took his enforcement duties with him everywhere; never relaxing until he was sure the bear clan was safe. Even then, he slept with one eye open.

Trey was the youngest brother and the playful one. He made it his purpose in life to stop by the café at least three times a day to check on her. Sometimes, it was to spend a few hours either sitting in a corner booth or fixing something. However, since his mate, Nichole, had become pregnant, he didn't leave the den for more than a few minutes at a time. So Ryan had been drafted to fill in on Trey's shift of watching out for her.

Tiffany smiled at Ryan as she noted the way he watched Kaylee. "Kay, why don't you sleep over at my place? I could use the help with the party, and with the storm coming, I don't want you to try and drive up in the snow.

From the corner of her eye, Tiffany saw Kaylee stiffen slightly before she replied. "I didn't pack a bag."

"No need. We're the same size, and I have plenty of clothes to share." Tiffany turned to the female. "Please. You, Nichole, Connie, and I will have so much fun. Besides, my mom has been wanting to see you again."

Kaylee glanced to Ryan, then quickly averted her gaze, her cheeks turning pink. She was the only human Tiffany knew of outside of the mates that knew about shifters. Tiffany was so glad that her father had allowed her to tell Kaylee about them. It made being her friend easier and yet harder at the same time. While Tiffany didn't age, Kaylee did. That saddened Tiffany because if she didn't find her friend a mate, she'd have to watch Kaylee grow old, and could possibly lose her.

"Please," Tiffany asked again, batting her lashes.

Kaylee laughed. "Okay, I'll come."

"Yay!" Tiffany pulled her into a tight hug.

"Not so tight, sister bear."

Releasing Kaylee, she drew back and scanned her human friend for injuries while her heart beat wildly. "I'm so sorry."

A small, shy laugh escaped Kaylee. "No harm done." She glanced to Ryan and quickly lowered her gaze.

Curious, Tiffany cut her brother a narrowed-eyed gaze. He stared at Kaylee as if unsure; as if he were battling with his inner demons. Tiffany frowned. The latter may be the case. After all, he had tied himself to a demon to save her life.

Tiffany didn't know all the details. Ryan refused to talk about it, especially with her.

However, the more she studied him, the more she realized he was attracted to Kaylee. Hiding her smile, she focused back on her friend. "Can you help Ryan load the cake?" She turned to her brother. "Be very careful with that cake. I don't have time to make another one."

He reached over the counter and ruffled her hair. "Yes, little sis."

She playfully pushed his hand away. "I mean it. I'll hurt you if something happens to that cake."

"Nothing will happen to it. I already have a space for it in the back seat of the truck." Ryan nodded at Kaylee to lead the way to the walk-in refrigerator. When the two of them disappeared into the kitchen area, Tiffany shook her head and gathered the two boxes she'd packed.

She could definitely see Kaylee with Ryan. The only problem would be how to get his demon mark removed so he would be free to choose a mate. With it, he was bound to the demon, and one day, that bastard would come for Ryan and take him away from his family.

Fisting her hands after loading the boxes in the back of the truck, she made it her purpose to find out what it would take to release Ryan from the demon's contract. First she had a party to plan. She would not let anything dampen her holiday spirit and cheer.

After all, winter was her favorite season.

Entering the café, she glanced to the top shelf behind the counter. *There you are.* She'd thought she'd lost the cake topper or had accidentally thrown it out with last week's trash. For the life of her she couldn't remember where she'd put it.

She retrieved the step ladder from the back room as Ryan and Kaylee carefully carried the large cake out to the truck. Anxiety bubbled up inside Tiffany, and she fought the urge to go help, to make sure the cake made it safe and sound into the backseat. No, Ryan would be careful.

She really needed to get a handle on her need to control everything.

After setting the ladder in place, she climbed it and reached for the cake topper. It was a little farther out of reach than she'd thought. She stretched but lost her balance and fell, the ladder tumbling to the ground with her.

Pain shot up her leg from her ankle, then through her knee as it made contact with the floor. Tears stung her eyes as she cried out. Oh, please don't be broken. But she feared it was. Or at least it hurt as if it were.

"Tiffany!"

Ryan's shout held a tone of panic she'd heard in her brother's tone many times as she'd gotten into trouble over her thirty years of life. He knelt beside her and frowned. "Your ankle is broken."

"Thank you, Doctor Black." Tiffany rolled her eyes while ignoring the throbbing pain in her ankle and knee. "Just get me to Holt so he can heal me enough to work on the rest of the food."

Ryan shook his head but didn't comment. Smart man. She really didn't want to hear that she couldn't work. From anyone. The Winter Solstice and Anthony's mating ceremony would be perfect. She didn't care how much pain she was in. It was going to go on as planned. Period.

2

"It's broken."

Tiffany glared at Holt, who sat on the coffee table in her living room with her leg in his lap. "So, fix it."

The Healer shook his head. "It would be best to let it heal on its own."

Was he crazy? "I have a party to cater."

He worked his strong, masculine jaw while his bear flashed behind dark green eyes. Normally, Holt didn't show any aggression. He was, after all, a born Healer. And a powerful one, even without linking to the Alpha's magick. As the clan's princess, Tiffany knew all too well that he could heal her broken bones.

There was something primal about the male tonight. He seemed more protective, more on edge than she'd ever seen him. He let out a low growl. "I *could* set the bone, but the muscles need time. It's best to let your bear do that."

She opened her mouth to argue, but her mother entered from the front door and sent Tiffany a warning glare. "Tiffany, don't be stubborn. You have Kaylee, Connie, Nichole, and me here to help. Plus, we'll get the boys to pitch in."

Tiffany sagged in her seat and folded her arms. Nothing was going to work out as she'd envisioned. Once you got too many cooks in the kitchen, all hell broke loose. Too many ideas and changes. Focusing back on Holt, Tiffany smirked. If the Healer wouldn't do his quick fix, then he was going to help her in the kitchen. That way, her sisters-in-law and mother could help with decorations and other minor details.

"Okay, Mom. You, Connie, and Nichole can help with party specifics and setup. Holt will be helping Kaylee and me with the food."

Holt's grip on her thigh tightened slightly before he met her stare, terror lighting up his gaze. "I can't cook."

"Can you follow directions and a recipe?"

He glanced to her mom, then back to her. "Yes…"

"Then it's settled. Since I have to heal on my

own and be off my feet for most of the next couple of days, then you are helping me with the food."

She held Holt's gaze for several long seconds. The green in his eyes faded from dark to the light and back to dark again. Images of him naked right before he shifted into his black bear flashed in her mind. Heat rose up from deep within. She'd always thought the Healer was hot, but in that moment, he was so much more.

He was her mate.

Damn.

His sage scent intensified as he leaned forward, apparently forgetting that they weren't alone. Once his lips touched hers, she was lost. The whole world could crumble around them and she wouldn't care. In that moment, all she wanted was him, deep inside of her.

When she moved her leg, intending to wrap both of them around his hips, pain chased all sensual desires away. She hissed, holding back a scream. Holt was quick to soothe the pain by wrapping his large, strong hands gently around her ankle. Warm, electric pulses vibrated through her foot, ankle, and up her leg.

Within moments, she felt better. A low growl from the doorway drew her attention. She turned her head and saw her brothers taking up the space. A moment later, Connie and Nichole pushed their way into the now cramped living room. Really? She'd broken her ankle. It wasn't like she'd died. "Why don't you call the rest of the clan? I'm sure we could squeeze them all in."

Her mom laughed but turned to her brothers. "Boys, you will handle all the lifting and get the tables and chairs and anything else Tiffany needs you to do. Right now, she needs to rest. Tomorrow we'll get to work on the party."

Her mother shooed them out of the house. Before leaving, she turned to Tiffany. "Call me if you need anything."

"I will. Thanks, Mom."

Tiffany glanced to Kaylee, who sat quickly in a chair, watching them all. It looked like she felt out of place. Frowning, Tiffany asked no one in particular, "Want to make hot cocoa and s'mores?"

Holt gently placed her now bandaged ankle atop a pillow on the coffee table. "I'll start a fire in the fireplace."

"I'll get the fixings for the s'mores. Nichole makes better cocoa than me," Connie announced before the two females disappeared into the kitchen.

Studying Kaylee, Tiffany smiled. "Are you okay?

I didn't mean to drag you here to put up with my crazy family for the gods know how long."

Instantly, Kaylee relaxed and returned her smile. "Your family isn't crazy." Her smile faded and she averted her gaze to the fire Holt was starting. "At least you have a family."

Tiffany's heart ached for her friend. "I thought you had an aunt you were close with."

Kaylee shrugged. "We're not as close as I pretend to be."

Just then, Connie and Nichole entered the room with their loot. The smell of chocolate was heavenly. Even though Tiffany wanted to tell everyone to leave so she and Kaylee could talk more, she knew that the human needed to be around friends. And if she thought she didn't have family, she was mistaken. Tiffany had included her in her family the moment they'd met. Kaylee just didn't know that yet.

Holt stood and faced Tiffany, his features masked. "I'll come by in the morning." Then he left.

Tiffany stared at the closed door for several moments. What the hell was that? Did he not feel the mating pull?

Nichole sat beside her after placing the marshmallows, graham crackers, and chocolate on the coffee table. She patted her hand and gave it a gentle squeeze. "He likes you."

Tiffany straightened. "Who?"

Connie laughed. "Holt. He couldn't get out of here fast enough."

"What? Did you not just see that he rejected me?"

Kaylee shook her head. "Even I could see he wasn't rejecting you. He was fleeing."

"Yep, not to mention the huge erection he had." Nichole laughed harder.

Connie snorted. "Yes. The poor bear is probably heading to his house to take a cold shower."

Confused, Tiffany glanced back at the door. She had apparently missed something. Sure she'd felt the heat and passion that had ignited between them during the kiss. But if he'd felt the mating urge, wouldn't he have wanted to act on it? "Why would he leave, then?"

"Because he's a male. We all know most males have commitment issues." Connie prepped the marshmallows for the fire while Nicole topped off the cocoa with whipped cream and grated hazelnuts.

"But he's my mate."

Nichole handed her a cup. "Then we'll help you snag him."

3

She's my mate.

Holt stepped out of the shower, tugged the towel from the rack, and wrapped it around his hips. He'd known Tiffany all her life. Sure, he'd noticed that she had become a beautiful woman. But he'd never felt the urge to mate with her until he'd looked into her blue eyes an hour ago.

For a brief moment, their bears had connected. Then the tiny threads of a bond had appeared. When he'd kissed her... Fuck. He'd had to get out of there. Clear his head.

The space between them and the long shower had only made the urge grow stronger. A growl rumbled from him. He ran a hand through his wet hair. What was wrong with him? He was no alpha male. As the Healer, he relied on his compassion and empathy to heal others. It wasn't like him to turn into a protective, growling male.

He crossed the living room and stopped mid-step when he reached the door on his way to the kitchen. Trey's and Anthony's scents reached his awareness a moment before a hard knock sounded from outside.

After two strides, he jerked the door open. Anthony held up two twelve-packs, one in each hand, and grinned. Trey was the one who spoke. "We thought you might want some company and a beer or four."

Holt grunted and moved away from the doorway, allowing them entry into his home. The Healer's home had always been an open door for the den, so he was surprised the males had knocked. "Why do you two think I need company?"

Anthony put the beer in the icebox and laughed. "Unless that kiss you laid on our sister was a new healing technique, I'm guessing you will be joining the family soon. Of course, that means we have to put you through the third-degree before Dad gets to you."

Holt dropped into one of two soft, brown leather armchairs, not caring that he was still in his towel. It wasn't like nudity was an issue among shifters. Plus, he was the same age as Anthony. They'd grown up together. And, Holt had healed each of their asses on more than a few occasions.

He was about to reply to Anthony's taunt when two more knocks sounded on the door, and it opened to reveal Ryan. The male's short hair looked as if he'd tried to pull it out while his blue eyes appeared almost black. A hum of dark power rippled through his aura.

Either he had just come from a visit with the demon who'd marked him, or he was being called to a meeting. Holt could never tell one way or the other. The level of dark energy felt the same to him.

Giving Ryan a short nod, Holt asked, "Everything okay?"

"Fine."

The word was clipped as Ryan went to the kitchen. He returned a moment later with a beer and leaned against the wall next to the door.

Holt sighed. "Tiffany is my mate." He held up a hand, stopping them from speaking all at once. "What I don't understand is why now? Why not when she came of age?"

The thought of her going through her first heat cycle with another male bothered him more than it should. Before he hadn't cared…much, who the male was that had taken care of her urges.

Trey sat on the sofa and let out a low chuckle. "Before you break the arms off that chair, I thought you should know that Tif opted for meds during her heat cycle."

Holt snapped his gaze to Trey. "Who gave them to her?"

She should have come to him. He was the Healer.

"Calm your fucking bear. Your mother gave them to her," Anthony said with the power of his Marshal status, which was pretty damn close to the level of power the Alpha held. The flow of energy filling the room calmed him, but only a little.

Holt closed his eyes and rested his head against the chair. "I don't know how to handle this need to..."

He let his words fade away. After all, they were her brothers and didn't need to hear what his mind and the bear were planning to do to her when they got her alone.

"What if she doesn't accept you?" Ryan said from the door. There was no emotion in the male's tone. No way of knowing if he was baiting Holt or not.

"Does that actually happen?" Holt stated, almost as calmly.

Silence fell between them for a few moments

before Anthony spoke. "It has. One mate can feel the pull, but the other doesn't."

Holt frowned. What if Tiffany didn't feel the pull? The thought of her rejecting him and his bear made a new fear rise up. He couldn't stay in the den if she chose not to mate him. The jealousy associated with watching her mate another would drive him insane.

He let out a low growl. "How do I woo her?"

Anthony laughed. "Her passion is her café and her love for cooking and baking. You have to learn to like it, too. And understand that, mate or not, she will put Beary Sweets above all."

He nodded. He liked to cook. Baking was another thing. It was too scientific for him. But he could learn. Tiffany was the perfect one to teach him.

4

Tiffany eased out of bed, slowly putting her weight on her feet. She'd slept in bear form, hoping to help her ankle heal a little faster. Relief washed over her as she stood and only had half the pain she'd had the night before. There was no way she'd be able to walk on the ankle for long, but she could manage. Especially when Holt arrived and she could wrap herself in his scent.

Her body warmed at the thought of him. His sage scent filled her mind, and she groaned as she hobbled to the door. Tiny shards of pain shot up her leg with each step, chasing away any desire she'd stirred at the thought of Holt.

Apparently, her bones hadn't healed as much as she'd hoped. No. Usually, breaks took twenty-four hours or more—in bear form—before they mended together. Tiffany didn't have that long. So she would deal with the discomfort.

She got halfway down the hallway when Kaylee exited the guestroom. "Tif, what are you doing? I told you to text me when you got up."

Waving the female off, Tiffany said, "I'm fine. It only hurts when I walk on it."

The scowl she got from Kaylee made her laugh and lose her balance. Kaylee rushed to her side and tucked her shoulder under Tiffany's arm for support. "Stop being stubborn."

Tiffany smiled and let her friend help her to the living room. Kaylee would make a good mate for Ryan. She had just the right amount of sass to put her brother in his place when needed. Plus, she had a huge heart. Only thing Tiffany had to do was figure out how to unbind him from that demon.

"What do you think about Ryan?"

Kaylee stiffened before answering. "He's quiet and sometimes seems standoffish."

Yep, that sounded like Tiffany's brother. "That's his shield he hides behind. You'll have to break it down."

After helping her sit on the sofa, Kaylee stood back up and held Tiffany's gaze. "What makes you think I want to break them down?"

A small laugh escaped Tiffany just as a knock sounded on the door. By the notes of sage in the scent, she knew it was Holt. "You can pretend to not want to, but I can sense otherwise."

Kaylee rolled her eyes as she turned to the door. All the while, the female's scent sharpened at the mention of Ryan. Tiffany was definitely going to find out how to get rid of that demon.

Right after Winter Solstice. At the moment, she had a sexy Healer to capture.

Meeting the scowl on Holt's face, Tiffany waved and smiled. "Hi, handsome."

"Please tell me you didn't walk out here on your own."

"Kay helped me."

Kaylee grunted. "After I found her in the hallway."

Tiffany folded her arms and pretended to be hurt. "Traitor." The urge to stick out her tongue at Kaylee died the moment Holt lifted her leg to examine her ankle. Heat traveled up her leg to other more sensitive parts.

She fought off a groan as she gazed into his green eyes. His bear flashed from within the depths, and his scent sharpened. Every part of her ached for him like her body was on fire from the inside out.

He let go of her leg and put some distance between them. The warmth from his touch disappeared, leaving her feeling cool. The urge to pout, or beg for him to touch her again hung around her, pushing her to make an ass out of herself. Or at least act like a spoiled brat.

Grow up, Tiffany. "Kay, can you get my notebook and a pen?"

The female nodded and left to retrieve Tiffany's notebook from the kitchen. Some of Tiffany's best planning was done on paper.

Focusing on Holt, she watched him start another fire and let her thoughts wander. Who was he besides the clan's Healer? What did he like? She frowned as the idea that he might not like curvy females entered her mind. *Okay, Tif, you're being ridiculous.* If he didn't like her, he wouldn't have kissed her, right?

She'd never been insecure about her curves. In fact, she loved everything about her body. As a shifter, she couldn't get the human illnesses and other ailments that came with an unhealthy lifestyle. Although not all humans who have a few extra pounds are unhealthy. Kaylee ate healthily and walked at least three miles every day with Tiffany.

The female was at her peak physical condition, for her.

And they were both beautiful, curvy women. So what was Holt's deal?

Holt stood, glanced at her, and then frowned. "I'll be right back."

When Kaylee came back with the notebook, Tiffany took it and asked, "Do you think Holt is gay?"

The female laughed as she dropped on the sofa beside Tiffany. "No."

"How can you be sure? And what's so funny?"

"He's hot for you."

Tiffany sharpened her gaze on her best friend. If Kaylee had extra abilities, then the female was holding out on Tiffany. That broke a very important friendship rule. "How do you know?"

"Because he started the fire to hide his erection from you."

Tiffany's jaw dropped. "No, he didn't."

Kaylee laughed some more and nodded. "He did."

Tiffany folded her arms and stared at the door. The Healer sure did a good job of keeping his feelings in check. Wait a minute! "You looked at my mate?"

Surprise lit up Kaylee's face, followed by a wave of embarrassment. "I... I didn't mean to look. It was hard to miss. Are all bears hung like that?"

Tiffany sucked on her lower lip to keep from smiling. After all, she was supposed to be upset that her BFF saw a hint of Holt's package before she did. She gripped the square, quilted pillow next to her and swung it at Kaylee, hitting her in the head. "I don't know. But I don't want you looking at mine."

Kaylee laughed, clearly picking up on Tiffany's teasing. "I promise to try."

Tiffany let out a playful growl. "Try real hard, or I'll tell Ryan you have the hots for him."

"I do not!"

"Oh, please. I've seen the way you look at him."

Kaylee jerked the pillow from her and whacked her with it. "Who wouldn't look? He's cute. But that doesn't mean I have the hots for him."

"Yeah, yeah. Keep telling yourself that."

Holt entered the house again and studied them with raised brows. Damn, he was sexy. Leaning into Kaylee, she whispered, "I hate you."

"No, you don't."

Holt shut the door while shaking his head as if he didn't want to know what they were talking about. He was right. He didn't want to know.

Glancing to his hand, she spied a crutch. Excitement and fear fluttered inside her. He was giving her a way to get around the house. She would have independence. Then again, he could be backing out of helping her with the food.

He handed her the crutch and smiled. "I know how you love your independence and control over things. I thought this would make things easier." He held out a hand to help her stand. When she placed the crutch under her arm, he closed the distance and said, "Just don't use it on me when I screw up a recipe or two."

Her heart bloomed. He was staying to help. And she would get to spend time with him, tease him, and claim him as hers. "I'll try to behave."

His sensual, kissable lips lifted at the corners. "Ditto."

Holy fuck. Her heart pounded, and her blood raced through her veins. Why hadn't she realized how hot he was before now? Oh, yeah. She'd been busy with Beary Sweets, and never paid attention to much outside of the café.

Well, she was paying attention now, and she liked where it was going. "Alrighty, then, let's get started. I really just need you to help Kay prep for me."

He folded his arms and set his jaw. *Here it comes.* "You can prep and instruct me on cooking or whatever it's called."

Refraining from rolling her eyes, she narrowed her gaze at him. "The prep is more moving, lifting, and standing than stirring the ingredients and putting stuff in the oven."

His bear flashed in his eyes again before he glanced to Kaylee, who shrugged while trying to hide her amusement. Turning his attention back to Tiffany, he relaxed and stepped aside for her to pass. "Very well, you cook. But when I say you rest, you do just that."

Yes, my mate. A giggle bubbled up at the thought. He was hers, and she was willing to do anything he asked, follow him anywhere. However, did he feel the same?

5

When Holt arrived, he'd smelled the hint of pain. Her ankle was a little swollen, but healing as he'd expected. Tiffany was young and strong. The ankle would be healed almost completely by tomorrow morning. As long as the stubborn female stayed off it.

He watched Tiffany make her way to the kitchen. Her hips didn't quite sway due to the crutch she used, but her curves still begged for his hands. Stifling a groan, he followed her to the kitchen island and pulled out a high-back barstool. "Sit."

She smiled at him as she complied. The intense need that boiled his blood every time he looked into her blue eyes was going to kill him. Not to mention that his self-control was in jeopardy of snapping at any moment.

Kaylee laid the notebook and pen in front of Tiffany and sat on the stool beside her. Tiffany opened it to a page she had marked with a pink tab. "Since my father and brothers will be hunting for the meat, all we have are side dishes and dessert. Kay and I have several finger foods listed, and she's making her mixed berry tarts."

Holt studied the list. Even though it was upside down to him, he could read the items. Pointing at the words cranberry stuffing, he asked, "Is that your mom's secret recipe?"

"It is, plus a few extras I've added."

Mesmerized, he stared into her blue depths. Glee and mischief mingled together as if she were plotting world domination. *She just might be.*

There was so much he didn't know about her. "I can't wait to taste it."

Her face lit up, her bear flashing in her eyes. Almost as fast as the emotion appeared, it was gone. She glanced at her notebook and opened it to the last page, where several index cards were tucked into a small pocket. Pulling them out, she shifted through them until she found the one she searched for and handed it to him. "Gather the ingredients and bring them here. I'll help chop the veggies and fruit."

Nodding, he studied the card then pulled the

items from the oversized, double door refrigerator. When he dropped his loot on the island countertop, Kaylee brought over a couple of knives then moved to the kitchen counter to start her tarts.

He lifted one of the knives and raised a brow to Tiffany. "Is there any specific way you want them cut?"

She shrugged. "Not too big or too small. One of Mom's secrets is that she leaves the stuffing kind of chunky, especially the fruit and nuts."

"Got it." He began with the onion while Tiffany grabbed the cranberries.

They worked in silence except for the occasional instructions from Tiffany. Holt didn't mind the silence, though. He'd gotten lost in listening to Tiffany's steady breathing, and her soothing voice. Besides, her intoxicating, berry scent calmed him as he helped with the food prep.

In the few hours they'd worked, he'd briefly forgotten that Kaylee was there until she placed a dozen small glass bowls with lids in front of him. The human female had been working quietly a few feet away. Then again, Holt's attention had been fixed on Tiffany.

He glanced to the clock and was amazed to see that they'd worked right through lunch. It was going on 3:00 p.m. Wow, how had he not noticed the time?

Turning his attention back to Tiffany, he knew how. She was beautiful, and he found it was too easy to lose himself around her. To her. A few thick strands of her black hair had escaped her ponytail and framed her slightly round face. The contrast of her dark hair against her milky skin made his hands itch to touch her. Then his eyes fell to her pouty, kissable lips. It took all of his self-control to not drag her across the island and kiss her senseless.

A knock on the door snapped Holt from his thoughts. A moment later, Connie and Madison—Tiffany's mom—entered with laughter in their eyes as if they'd recently shared a joke. However, Holt sensed something mischievous in the works.

Sure enough, his suspicions were confirmed when Madison spoke. "We've come to borrow Kaylee for the day."

Holt's heart hammered and his bear perked up, ready to finally be alone with Tiffany. But Tiffany appeared to be alarmed by the news. "Why? I need her here."

Mama Bear shrugged and gestured to Holt. "You have help. Plus, the girls and I are fixing a couple of sides to lighten your load."

By the way Madison glanced from him to Tiffany with a mixture of approval and glee, he knew what she was up to. It wouldn't surprise him if Kaylee didn't come back that night. *Thank you, Mama Bear.* "We can manage without Kaylee. In fact, I think we're almost done with the prep."

Tiffany glanced around the kitchen, completely avoiding his gaze. Then she dropped her shoulders and muttered, "I guess we did get a lot done this morning."

"Good." Madison turned to the door. "Come on, Kaylee, we have a lot to do."

Holt watched Tiffany as the other two females left. She stared at the door for several moments before reaching for the crutch where she'd rested it against the island next to her. Once her fingers touched it, it fell to the floor. He was on the other side of the counter before her feet hit the tile.

Instead of picking up the crutch, he scooped her up in his arms and carried her to the sofa. "Want anything to eat?"

"Yes, please. There are pre-portioned meals in the freezer."

He frowned, not at all liking the idea of her dieting. "What for?"

Tiffany laughed. "I get so busy working on new

recipes and with the day-to-day at the café, that when I settle down, I'm too tired to cook. So, once a week I cook all my meals for the week and freeze them."

His cheeks heated with embarrassment. "I'm sorry…"

She pressed a finger to his lips and gave him a smile that made his pants uncomfortable. "Shush. Go warm us up something to eat."

"Yes, ma'am." Before he straightened, he leaned in and kissed her. Pleasure exploded across his senses. When their tongues touched, a shot of electrified energy blasted through him.

Reluctantly, he ended the kiss and pressed his forehead to hers. A soft sigh escaped Tiffany. "If you have no intentions to claim me as your mate, you need to leave."

What? He drew back, confused, and stared into her blue gaze. "Trust me, I have every intention, but I thought you needed time. That we needed time to…I don't know, date or something."

She nibbled on her bottom lip briefly before replying. "Dating is for humans. We've known each other all my life, even became friends. There's no one else I'd rather be mated to."

He scooped her up and proceeded down the hall, thoughts of food forgotten.

"Where are you taking me?"

By the slight tremble in her voice and the smile on her lips, he guessed she already knew the answer. However, he loved the way her cheeks colored when he teased her. "I'm taking you to your room so I can claim you."

As he suspected, she didn't back down. No, not his Tiffany. She wrapped her arms around his neck and bit his earlobe before whispering, "I accept all of you, forever."

His cock jerked and his soul filled with notes of her. Her acceptance had started the mating bond. The only thing left to do was take her, which he planned to do. All night long.

∾

Tiffany watched Holt as he laid her on the bed and tore off his shirt. Hard muscles flexed with each movement, making her mouth water. He was hers, and he wanted her for his mate. Briefly, the thought that everything was happening too fast entered her mind, but she shoved it away.

All her life, she'd dreamt of the day she would mate. And to find a mate in a friend was icing on her cupcakes. She'd grown to admire, respect, trust, and even love Holt over her lifetime. Until the day before, when she'd felt the tug to him, she'd only seen him as a close friend. Right then, she knew it was so much more. They were fated mates.

His mouth claims hers in another toe-curling kiss. Pleasure burned in her belly and spread to more sensitive areas. Her skin heated and she ached for his touch. As if knowing what she needed, he traced his hand over her hip to the hem of her shirt. With quick efficiency, he removed her tee and bra then set upon her jeans.

"I want to take it slow, but not sure if I can this first time."

"Then don't," she pleaded, needing to feel him inside her. "I'm already wet."

His sexy mouth lifted and one brow raised as he slid his hand down her belly and sank his fingers into her folds. A gasp escaped as desire she'd never felt before flared to life, threatening to consume every inch of her.

When he entered her with his fingers, she nearly came. Tingles of pleasure skittered over her and she moved her hips in tempo with his hand as he fingered her to an orgasm.

She cried out in complete bliss as the climax crashed over her, making her body jerk and twitch. Good gods, he was going to kill her with pleasure.

He quickly stripped the rest of the way and trailed kisses up her stomach to her breasts before taking one of her nipples into his mouth. Desire rolled within, building up for another wave of ecstasy. With his right arm, he lifted her leg and slowly pushed inside her. She fisted the sheets and sucked in a breath as pain and pleasure mingled, fueling the building climax.

Once buried deep inside her, he began to move, slowly at first then faster. She wrapped her arms around him, one hand in his hair and the other gripping his shoulder as they moved as one.

A scream ripped from her throat as a more intense orgasm exploded through her. Holt followed suit as he reached his own release.

Panting and feeling boneless, she hugged him tightly. "That was amazing."

"Yes. Now I know why men go crazy without their mates."

She laughed and looked inside herself, seeing the

mating bond weaving together, growing stronger and brighter by the moment.

They were mated.

Holt framed her face with his hands. "I never realized until yesterday that I love you so much more than a friend."

Her heart bloomed with glee and adoration. "I love you, too."

6

Everything blissfully ached and hummed at the same time. Tiffany smiled and stepped out of the shower, amazed at how much better her ankle felt upon waking that morning. Sex with the Healer really was good for the body.

Her smile died as a loud crash sounded from the front of the house. "What the hell?"

Grabbing her pink, plush robe, she slipped it on and rushed out of the bathroom to see Holt exiting the bedroom, naked. She briefly enjoyed the view as she followed him down the hall. Once in the living room, her heart dropped to her feet and her stomach soured. The ceiling over her kitchen had caved in. Snow, wood, and plaster were scattered everywhere.

She shivered and drew her robe tighter around her as she made her way to the kitchen to assess the damage. Holt followed and grabbed her hand in his. "Be careful."

"I will." She squeezed his hand.

The farther she crept into the kitchen, the sicker she felt. The whole roof had caved in on that corner of the house, right over the walk-in fridge. Dread slammed into her. *The cake*! Charging forward, she tossed debris out of her way and opened the fridge door. Sadness mixed with anger swirled inside of her. The cake that had once stood tall in the middle of the walk-in had been toppled over by a beam.

Over half of the shelves were broken off the walls, and all the prep work they'd done the day before was ruined. Gods, she wanted to cry. They'd never get everything done in time for the winter celebration in six hours.

Holt came up behind her and placed his hands on her shoulders. She sighed. "You better get dressed before my family walks in. She'd smelled her brothers when she entered the walk-in, their scents growing closer by the moment. As shifters, they didn't have an issue with being nude, but she didn't want to deal with her overprotective brothers and father, finding Holt naked in her destroyed kitchen.

"Yeah...I'll do that." He backed away then added,

"Come sit and wait for your family. We'll figure out how to fix this."

She wrapped her arms around her waist. There was no fixing this. Everything was ruined. Blinking the tears from her eyes, she left the fridge.

As she entered the living room, the front door swung open. Trey was the first to reach her side. "Are you okay?"

Absently she nodded, barely noticing her other two brothers and parents file into her house. A moment later, her sisters-in-law came in and tugged her to sit on the sofa. "We should go to Mom and Dad's."

Tiffany wasn't sure if it was Connie or Nichole who'd spoken, but whoever it was, she was right. The house was freezing. "I need to get dressed and gather some clothes."

Connie hugged her. "We'll come with you while the guys and Mom see what is salvageable."

Tiffany nodded and stood. Her mind worked over the quick recipes that would work as replacements for what was lost. She may be a little childish and a brat at times, but the one thing she was not, was a quitter. Sure it upset her to lose all the hard work, especially on the cake. But she would not give up. "We have a lot of work to do, and I'll need everyone's help."

Just then, Holt entered the living room. All eyes but hers turned to him, and silence filled the space. Tiffany wanted to hide under the couch or run out the door. Instead of growling, her brothers just sent the Healer a short nod before they headed toward the kitchen.

Meeting her mom's gaze, Tiffany said, "I'm confused."

Nichole laughed and tugged her to the bedroom. "Your brothers already grilled Holt."

"Apparently, while we had our girls' night here the other night." Connie smiled then grabbed Tiffany's overnight bag.

Figures. Her brothers couldn't let her live her life. That was probably the reason Holt had been so hesitant before they made love. "What did they say?"

The females glanced at each other for a moment before Nichole spoke. "Trey told me he sensed that Holt was a little freaked out about recognizing you as his mate. So he called Ant, who called Ryan."

"Since when do my brothers, who have chased all my boyfriends away before, start playing matchmakers?"

Connie smirked, shoving things into the

overnight bag. "Because they know how it is to find a mate, and how incredible it is to bond with them."

"Plus Holt is already part of the family from what I understand. He's the Healer, and his loyalty to your father will die with him." Nichole spoke from her seat on the bed beside Tiffany.

"I guess I thought they'd be mad..." She fell silent, letting everything sink in. There were so many emotions running rampant inside of her. But the one thing that stood out the most was her love for Holt. "We're mated."

"Yes, we know," the females said at once then giggled.

"How did that happen? Why did it take so long for us to feel the pull?"

Tiffany had scented her mother before she spoke from the doorway. "Sometimes, we need to be friends with our mates first."

Smiling, Tiffany nodded. She really didn't care about the hows or whys. The questions were on her mind because she didn't want to think about her destroyed house and cake. "I'm glad it worked out that way." Her chest swelled, but her mind kept going to Holt, then the mess in her kitchen. "First, we need to figure out what we're going to do about the food for tonight's Solstice/Mating ceremony."

Nichole patted Tiffany's hand. "Now we have three matings to celebrate."

Yes, they did. Tiffany smiled widely. Despite the way the morning had started out, the rest of the day and her life were going to be great.

7

"Winter is definitely here. Last night's storm dumped a lot of snow on us, and a few houses, my daughter's included, suffered some damage. But we pulled together and helped each other out. Like a strong clan should." Elijah Black's opening was warm and powerful.

Pride and love lingered in the air and in Holt's heart. Beside him, his mate leaned in. He hugged her closer and kissed the top of her head. "The food turned out great. Everyone is going to love it."

"Thanks. I'm still sad the beautiful cake didn't make it."

"But your cupcakes are amazing."

She laughed softly to not disrupt her father's Solstice speech. "Yeah, even though most of them aren't as pretty as others."

After the males had returned from hunting, they helped decorate the cupcakes. Tiffany frowned at them when they were finished, but didn't let it bother her. Or so she liked everyone to think. She was too OCD, and she couldn't hide it from Holt. They were mated now. Her emotions were his, and his, hers.

Elijah called to the newly mated pairs of his family. "As we welcome the birth of the sun god, I'm welcoming three new members to my family. I've gained two more daughters and another son over the last few months. Nichole, Connie, and Holt, welcome to the family."

The clan roared out their congratulations and clapped. The strength of the den intensified the magick within the circle they used for celebrations—like the one they held that night. Times like these were why Holt loved his clan so much. Now he had one more reason to love it. She stood by his side like she had all her life, now completely open to him.

Turning to her, he lifted her chin so she met his stare. "I love you, my mate."

She stood on her toes and kissed him quickly on the lips. "I love you, always and forever."

The End

BEAR MARKED

BEARS OF BLACKROCK, BOOK FOUR

Bear Marked

A demon owns his soul.

Bear shifter and youngest son of the Blackrock Clan Alpha, Ryan Black, refuses to tie another to the demon who marked him. A demon who claims to be his mate. And now, staying away from the curvy beauty, Kaylee Martin, tears at his heart.

Her secret could kill her.

Kaylee has loved Ryan from the moment she met him at his sister's café a few years ago. His boyish good looks and playful charm are only two of the reasons she's drawn to him. But admitting her feelings for the bear would expose a secret she's spent a lifetime protecting.

A demon with heart.

Adair doesn't fit into the demons' world and marking

his mate, Ryan, was the only way to protect him and his family. Kidnapping Ryan's sister to gain the bear's attention and trick him into the mating was the biggest mistake of Adair's life. When he sees Kaylee for the first time, he's confused. Two mates? However, Kaylee isn't what she pretends to be.

When demons threaten Kaylee's life, Ryan faces tough choices. He must learn to listen to the truth and forgive Adair, because working with the demon to protect their mate sparks a desire too strong to ignore.

1

The females were plotting against him, or for him, which would be the same thing in his case. However, their plot wouldn't work.

No one could free him from his mark. That was a destiny he'd have to face on his own. Like a ready-or-not kind of thing. The demon that tried to pull his strings wasn't going to let go without a fight.

Lifting his gaze from his tablet, he watched the curvy beauty, Kaylee, smile at customers as she took the orders behind the counter of Beary Sweets Cafe. She had dimples in her cheeks and big blue eyes that appeared haunted on too many occasions. Her long brown hair was pulled back in a ponytail. A couple of strands escaped to hang on either side of her face.

Ryan fought off a groan and the need to go over

and tuck the strands of hair behind her ears. And kiss her...

"Demons like to make deals. We'd have to trick him into taking one that releases Ryan from the bond." Connie, one of his new sister-in-laws, stated across the booth from him.

Why had he agreed to go to lunch with the females? Because Nicole was pregnant and her mate wouldn't let her out of the den unless she had a guard. And Ryan wasn't doing anything. Little did he know it was all part of their plan.

Females.

"Forget it. None of my family or clan will go anywhere near the demon. I volunteered for the mark." *I'll deal with the consequences.* He ground his molars as the mark behind his left ear burned. Another call from Adair. The male had been summoning him off and on for months. However, that morning the bastard had called every hour at first. In the last hour, the mark had become a constant burn.

Ryan hated to be called like a slave but if he didn't answer soon Adair would just show up.

"Because of me," Tiffany whispered beside him.

Ryan sighed and covered her hand. His heart broke because she blamed herself for the demon mark. "You're my baby sister. I'd do it a hundred times over to know you're safe and now happily mated." He released a breath and laid the tablet on the table and sat back, giving up on trying to ignore everyone around him. "Promise me, all of you, to let me handle it."

The mark burned hotter, more intense than it ever had before. Ryan rubbed the spot and growled. Time was up. He'd avoided the demon for too long. "Look. Just promise me not to go after me or the demon."

Tiffany let out a sigh that sounded like a soft sob. The next moment, Kaylee stopped at the table. "Another round of lattes?"

Ryan glanced up and their gazes locked for several moments. Recognition registered deep within. His bear pawed at him to reach out and touch her, taste her, claim her.

A yearning he could never act on stirred. *Damn, you demon.* He screamed the thought, hoping Adair would hear him.

Rising, Ryan picked up his tablet and walked to the door.

"Ryan? Ryan!"

The tremble in his sister's tone broke his heart. But what's done was done. He sealed his fate that day he offered to take Tiffany's place as the demon's mate. Nothing was going to change that not even the fact Kaylee was his destined mate.

When he exited the café, Adair was leaning against his truck, waiting. Ryan let out a growl, not liking the demon so close to his family. Yet, Ryan couldn't deny him anything. He'd like to blame it on the mark, the pact he made to keep Tiffany safe. He was in denial though. Adair was...dark, easy on the eyes, and another one of Ryan's potential mates.

Another growl rumbled from Ryan's chest as he stalked toward the tall, lean yet muscular male watching him with eyes the color of midnight. His hair fell over his shoulder in waves of black silk. Adair was definitely easy on the eyes and built for pleasing his lover.

Damn Demon.

Ryan didn't like to be forced into a loveless mating.

A few feet from Adair, Ryan sensed Kaylee behind him. Turning, he locked gazes with the female as she stood outside the café door. Beside him Adair moved toward her but Ryan gripped his arm. "Leave her alone."

Adair raised a dark brow, and one corner of his

mouth curled up. "She is *our* mate. Do you not see it?"

Damn it. Yes, he saw it, smelled it, and felt it with every fiber of his soul. Dragging Kaylee through a mating with a demon would be selfish. She deserved better than a life in hell. "She doesn't belong in your world."

"Have you let her make that choice?"

In a flash, Adair teleported to Kaylee's side. The demon locked gazes with Ryan. Fear made his heart pound like a jackhammer. No. Don't fucking do it. Not again. The demon gripped Kaylee by the arm and with a crooked grin the bastard dematerialized. *Fuck.* Ryan roared, rattling the windows of the café and the surrounding shops. His bear clawed at him from within, wanting out to kick the demon's ass.

Tiffany rushed outside, her eyes widened and face paled as she stared at the spot where Kaylee and Adair vanished. Tears filled her eyes as she turned her gaze to Ryan. His chest tightened and heart ached. Seeing his sister's terrified features broke him. It also fueled the need to set things straight with Adair. He took Kaylee to get his attention. Like he did with Tiffany.

Rushing to his sister, Ryan framed her face in his hands. "I'll get her back. He won't hurt her."

She shook her head, her eyes filled with tears. "How do you know that?"

Ryan closed his eyes briefly. He kept too many secrets from his family, yet he couldn't share any of them until he figured out what was really going on. "Trust me, please." When she nodded he kissed her forehead then handed her the keys to his truck. "Take the others to the den. I'll be there as soon as I can."

He didn't give her a chance to argue before he teleported to Adair's home in the Ever After. Materializing in the living room, Ryan met Adair's smug look. He growled and scanned the room. "Where's Kaylee?"

"She's unharmed."

Ryan fisted his hands and stepped closer to the demon. "I told you to leave her alone."

"What is yours is mine."

"That is not part of the deal." Fury rose up. His bear roared in his head. It was hard to keep the beast inside.

Adair waved a hand in the air as if to dismiss Ryan, then turned toward the kitchen. "Things have changed."

Bastard. The demon was insane if he thought Ryan would freely give him humans to do what he wished with. "No. You don't get to change things. I said my family is off limits. Kaylee is on the leave the fuck alone list."

Kaylee appeared in the opening of the hallway, arms wrapped around her stomach and her face as pale as white paint. "Ryan? I don't feel well."

His heart dropped to his feet as fear raced through him like a wildfire. He crossed the room with the inhuman speed he got from his bear and the connection to the demon. "What did you do to her?"

"She is sick from the teleportation."

"And from being here." Ryan took Kaylee by the hand and led her to the sofa.

Here was neither Earth nor Hell, but a space in between. Adair called it the Ever After, but his sister-in-law, Connie—who was a witch—called it the astral plane.

"This will ease the nausea." Adair offered Kaylee a mug with some kind of thick liquid in it.

Ryan jumped to his feet and slapped the mug from the demon's hand. The ceramic cup shattered on the floor, the contents spilling out. "She will not drink anything from you. I'm taking her home."

"I wouldn't poison our mate."

With a growl, Ryan faced Kaylee. When he reached out to her, pain exploded in his head and his mark burned like it never had before. Falling to his knees, he held his head and tried to will away the searing fire on his neck.

Squeezing his eyes shut, he pushed the pain through the link that connected him to Adair. The mark flared again and that time it was as if someone set his whole body on fire. *Fuck. Me.*

Opening his eyes, he glanced to Kaylee. Her brows were drawn and angry creases formed in her forehead. She jumped up as she yelled, "Stop! You're hurting him."

Breathing throw the pain, Ryan pushed to his feet. He focused on Kaylee as she knelt beside him. With a cool touch of her hand on his forehead, the throbbing in Ryan's skull eased a little.

A sigh sounded from Adair, who had sat on the sofa sipping his tea or whatever the hell he drank. "I've tried to get you to listen to me. Explain things."

Another growl rumbled from Ryan. He didn't care what Adair had to say. It wouldn't change the fact that he kidnapped Tiffany just to gain his attention. At least that was what the demon claimed.

"Nothing you say will change how I feel about you." Ryan edged closer to Kaylee, then wrapped his arms around her waist and teleported them out of there.

They took form in Kaylee's living room. It was the first thing he thought of. Kaylee dug her nails into his arm. "Oh, god I'm going to be sick."

He framed her face so she would focus on him. "Deep breaths. In one, two...out, three, four. That's it." He pressed his forehead to hers. "I'm so sorry. I never meant for you to get involved."

"Don't apologize." Her big blue eyes sparked with a knowing he hadn't noticed before.

With his extra senses, he picked up on something dark. Like a veil dropping away, her body vibrated with power. He stepped back, confused. "You're part demon?"

"Half demon. The only one who knows, besides you, is Connie. She told me to never tell Tiffany. I didn't understand why until your family talked about your mark." She averted her gaze.

"Why do you hide it? I mean, you've been friends with Tiffany for years. You even mask your power." Frowning, Ryan opened his senses, while careful to keep Adair out of his mind. Impossible to do with the bond of the mark.

His beautiful, curvy mate turned her back. A hint of fear mixed with anxiety flowed from her. He was about to demand her to explain but stopped when she spoke softly. "I can't let anyone know who and what I am. The demons have a price on my head."

Suspicion crawled up his spine. "Why?"

She glanced to him, her eyes shiny and the corners of her lips dipped. "I'm not supposed to exist. I'm half angel as well as half demon."

"Does Adair know? Is that why he took you?"

She shook her and gave her back to him. He cursed, feeling like an ass. Opening his mouth to tell her he didn't mean to offend her. That he was just trying to understand what the hell was going on.

The words never got a chance to leave his mouth. Kaylee sighed. Or was that a sob? "I don't think so. He might have picked up on my power even though I shield it. Maybe he didn't sense it. I don't know." She turned. Tears flowed down her cheeks and she started to shake. "The demons can't know about me. They will use me...kill me for my powers."

Unable to stand the fear in her eyes any longer, he crossed the small distance between them and pulled her into his arms. "We'll figure this out."

She nodded her head against his chest. They fell silent. After a long few moments, she asked, "What does Adair want with you?"

Should he tell her? Would she judge him for going along with it? Did any of it even matter anymore? After all she did just reveal her secret to him. "Adair believes I'm his mate."

"And you don't?"

The slight stutter in her tone drew his attention back to her face. "No. I mean…I could be attracted to him. But the way he's gone about getting my attention was a deal breaker. He used Tiffany to get to me, because he knew I would take her place."

Ryan sank down on the sofa and leaned forward, resting his elbows on his knees and his head in his hands. The mark on his neck burned again, telling him Adair was closing in. And he wasn't happy.

Yeah, Ryan sensed the demon's anger the moment he flashed them to her place. Damn why did he choose there of all places? He stood and grabbed her hand, "We have to go."

When she stared at him wide-eyed and nodded like she too sensed Adair close by, he flashed them to the one place he was sure Adair couldn't reach them —an old church he bought after being marked.

Taking form in front of the small, steepled building, he sensed Kaylee tense up beside him. She shook her head. "Why are we here?"

"I'm hoping to buy some time. Try to figure out what to do next." Ryan linked his fingers with

Kaylee's and paced toward the entrance of the sanctuary.

A cool, gentle hand touched his arm. When he stopped and faced her, Kaylee cupped his cheek and rose on her toes. "I don't need a protector. At least not one that wants to hide me."

His muscles tensed and he opened his mouth to argue with her and remind her he was a bear-shifter. It was his job to protect his mate...only she couldn't be his. Ever.

Before he got the words out, she pressed her lips to his. A fierce, primal need unraveled from deep within. He wrapped his arms around her, meshing her curves to him. Damn, she fit perfectly like his missing puzzle piece. And she tasted sweeter than his imagined. Honey and cinnamon. Holding her close, he slipped his tongue between her lips. A soft groan escaped her.

Much too soon, she broke the kiss. "I've wanted to do that since the first time I saw you."

"What made you so sure I'd kiss you back?" He couldn't help but tease her. The blush in her dimpled cheeks was his reward.

"I've known you for about seven years now. I've had some time to gather my courage."

A chuckle rumbled out. Gazing into her dark

blue eyes, he caressed her cheek with his knuckles. "He's not going to let me out of the mating. Besides, right now he's pretty pissed."

Her sensual lips lifted. "He now has his sights on mating both of us."

Ryan drew back slightly. "You know?"

"I think it has to do with the demon blood in my veins, but I know. I know you are mine. As is Adair." Kaylee sighed and pressed a finger to his lips when he opened his mouth. "Don't argue."

The demand in her tone made him hard. He wondered if she'd be just as demanding in bed. Opening his lips, he drew her finger inside. She gasped and pulled it away, which made him chuckle. "Here I thought you were timid."

She narrowed her eyes. "I don't have a timid bone in my body."

"I don't want you anywhere near Adair." A growl tore from his chest.

She pursed her lips and stared at him for several long moments. "And you don't get to make that choice for me. I'm part demon. Yes, Adair needs to work on his people skills and we will work on those. But I do know one thing that Adair might not."

"What?"

The shy smile returned before she answered.

"Demons become more human when they fall in love."

Confusion made Ryan draw back and study her features. "So mating for a demon isn't out of love?"

"No. It's more for status. However, for some reason Adair wants you, which will do nothing but get him kicked out of hell." She scanned the room then fixed her attention on the door. "You do know that most demons can still enter a church?"

They can? "Adair can't."

She lifted her gaze and locked it with his. "You sure?"

Ryan shrugged, took her hand, and tugged her close. "He doesn't go inside when he tracks me here. He stands outside and yells at me. Then uses the mark to make me come out."

Kaylee pursed her lips. "Control thing. He's playing with you. Demons are turned on by power plays. That will need to stop. We need to confront him and find out what he gains from mating us."

Ryan didn't like that she put herself in the mating but something told him not to argue. Frowning at her, he asked, "How do we do that?"

"We set the rules. If he truly believes we are his mates, then he'll abide by them."

Ryan wasn't so sure he liked where this was going. He crossed his arms. "What if he doesn't?"

Kaylee smiled. "Then he is lying and is fucking with you for personal gain. If that is the case we'll find a way to kill him."

His female was hot when she set a plan in place. But still. "How are you so sure?"

She rolled her eyes. "My dad is a demon. He told me when a demon falls in love he becomes more human. Just as he did when he met my mom. They now live here in the human world."

Shaking his head, he still didn't like her around Adair or plotting against him. It was too dangerous, too risky. Yet, the determination in her eyes hit him in the chest. He couldn't tell her no. Only support her decision and protect her.

After several moments she tugged his arms, unfolding them so she could link her fingers with his. "I'm not letting you go no more than you want to let me go."

His lips twitched. God, she was beautiful. "What kind of rules do we set for a demon?"

2

Adair let out a roar. The bear thought he'd run away from his fate.

Ever since Adair saw Ryan ten years ago he knew he had to have him. The physical ache for release was almost too much. Yet the bear rejected him.

And the male was blind to the danger he was in. Even after Adair tried to warn him and keep him safe, Ryan refused to listen.

Closing his eyes, he searched for the mark that bound them together. The same mark that allowed Adair to feel Ryan's storm of emotions. They went from anger to desire and back to anger like a continuous loop. Didn't he know it'd be easier to just let the mating happen?

Then the female entered their life. A half-breed

at that. Even though she hid it to blend in with the humans. That kind of control was taught from birth. Adair wanted to find out who her teacher was.

Kaylee intrigued him more than anyone had, even more than Ryan.

Focus, damn it. He cleared his mind and focused on locating his mates. When he found them, he growled. They were at that damned church.

Before he could teleport to the location, the air in his house electrified. The scent of sulfur and rain filled his senses, drawing a deep, fierce growl from him. The other demon materialized a few feet in front of him.

Adair snarled and fists his hands. "Malbhor."

A slow curl of the other demon's lips annoyed the fuck out of Adair. "Don't be so surprised to see me, brother."

"We aren't brothers. Not anymore." Adair had severed the tie to Malbhor and their insane father when the two of them went on a soul-stealing, demon-killing spree through Hell, that set Ryan and his family in their path.

They may be demons, but they also lived by rules set forth by Lucifer. The number one rule was to leave the humans alone to kill themselves.

"What do you want, Malbhor?"

"The female."

Adair barely contained his fury. "What female?"

Malbhor laugh, throwing his head back. "You know the one. Half demon, curvy, and smells delicious."

After he spoke the last words, Malbhor licked his lips. Adair flew at him, gripping him by the throat, and slamming him against the wall, leaving an imprint in the drywall. Fury ran in his veins like electrified fire. A growl ripped from his throat. "You will not touch her."

A dark brow rose as Malbhor taunted him further. "She's a descendant of Lucifer. The daughter of one of his sons."

Adair kept his surprise hidden. His brother was known to lie just to piss Adair off.

Normally he'd spar with Malbhor and tell him what an idiot he was for thinking about taking the female against her will. Especially if she truly was who he said. Lucifer would kill Malbhor on sight for touching the female.

"Good-bye, Malbhor." With all the bottled-up frustration from dealing with Ryan and the anger at the idea of what Malbhor would do to the female, Adair blasted his brother with his dark power. The male vanished. Most likely going back to dear ol' dad to lick his wounds. And his pride.

Worry set in, fueling his anxiety and need to get to his mates. Not knowing what his brother was up to or why he was so interested in Kaylee pissed him off. Adair needed to know the truth.

Connecting to the link he shared with Ryan, Adair teleported outside the church. He wasn't surprised to find his mates waiting for him. Ryan's arms crossed over his chest, making his broad shoulders wider. He narrowed his blue eyes and Adair hardened. The bear was hot but what was hotter was Kaylee standing behind him, her fingers curled around his large biceps. Her brown hair was still pulled back in a ponytail.

Seeing them together undid him on a level he never thought possible. In more ways than he dared to admit. However, their lives were in danger. Because of him and because of who Kaylee might be.

"Who is your father?" he asked Kaylee a little sterner than he intended.

She didn't flinch at his tone. Instead she pursed her lips, stood a little taller, and glared before finally replying to his question. "First we make a deal."

A deal? He almost laughed. "That old trick only works on weak minds."

She stepped around Ryan, fire in her eyes. Oh how he wanted to spar with her. Ryan snaked his arms around her and drew her back against him. Kaylee rolled her eyes. "So there are lesser demons with strong minds?" He let out a growl and she held up a hand to silence him. "Listen to me. We know you act all big, bad, mean demon, but we also know you don't know better. It's how demons are raised in Hell. To take what they want with no questions and never accept no as an answer."

She was beautiful, fiery, and full of passion. Her words hit him in the chest. "You are my mates. Of course I wouldn't take no for an answer."

She nodded while a humorless laugh escaped her. "And how has that worked for you with Ryan?" Shaking her head, she wiggled her finger at him. "You have to convince his bear by proving you are a worthy mate. I can guess the bear didn't like you stealing his sister away."

Adair winced. The she-demon did have a point. However, it was all he knew. Humans were too soft. "How else was I to get his attention?"

Ryan sneered at him and shuffled a protesting Kaylee behind him. "Kidnapping Tiffany only made me hate you more."

An ache started in his heart and cooled his blood.

His words cut deep because his emotions running along the bond said he spoke the truth. What had he done?

Adair turned, giving them his back.

Rustling and a soft slap of skin were followed by Kaylee saying, "Trust me."

Adair forced himself to remind still. He didn't need to see Ryan's rejection again. A moment later Kaylee's cool fingers touched his forearm. He glanced down and stared into her big blue eyes. "I don't understand. I didn't harm her."

Kaylee sighed. "When my mother taught me of the humans' way of life she told me to forget everything I was taught in my young life as a demon. Even though humans fight and at times act much like demons do, they live life with their hearts." She placed a hand over his heart and pressed. "I know you feel it. Love makes us all do crazy things. Humans can also forgive, and demons can be redeemed."

A ripple of white magic danced in her eyes. White magic? "Who is your mother?"

She shook her head and backed away. On impulse, Adair grabbed her hand. Ryan growled and was at his side in an instant. Kaylee held up a hand. "He's not hurting me." Then she met Adair's stare.

"Why should I tell you right now? You also have to earn my trust as well."

"If you are who I think, then your life is in more danger than I thought. And I'm the only one to keep both of you safe." He released her and straightened his spine.

∽

Kaylee eyed the demon. There was no way Adair had guessed who her parents were. If he knew who her mother was, then he'd know which of Lucifer's sons was her father. If anyone found out she'd be killed right after she was tortured while repaying her father's debt.

"There's only one demon in the last five centuries to mate with an angel."

Hugging her own waist, she shook her head and stepped back. "You can't...I can't."

Every part of her shook and fear burned her insides. She had to leave. Go into hiding, again.

Ryan appeared in her line of sight. He framed her face. "What's going on?"

Tears filled her eyes. "They will come for me. If word gets out..."

"No one will touch you." Both guys said at the same time. Even though their tone held a lethal protectiveness, it still didn't put her at ease.

Then Adair said, "We shouldn't talk here."

He grabbed Kaylee's and Ryan's hands. Ryan snatched his hand from Adair's. "You can't just teleport us around. Where are you taking us?"

Adair let out a low growl. Kaylee shivered and patted Ryan's arm. "He's right. We can't talk here." She met Adair's gaze. "If you led them to me, I'll bargain for you to take my place."

Adair winced. "I didn't. Please, come to my house. I have it warded and secure."

Kaylee's chest tightened. Aw, the demon was trying to be more human, which meant he was falling in love with Ryan. Taking Ryan's hand in hers, she gave a gentle squeeze. "Please. I'll explain everything when we get there."

He glanced to Adair and frowned, creasing his forehead. His bear flashed in his eyes. She wasn't sure if it was out of anger or fear. God, she hoped he could forgive her for withholding information about who her parents were from him.

3

Kaylee sat on a leather sofa in the living room of Adair's home. She hadn't expected him to have a house in the human realm. It was homey, clean, and comfortable. The one he took her to earlier that night was in Ever After, which also made her believe he was trying to separate himself from his demon heritage. Interesting.

Beside her, Ryan linked his fingers with hers. "I wonder what he did with the owners of this house."

A laugh burst from Kaylee before she could stop it. She jabbed Ryan in the side. "Hush. This is his home. There are no other scents in here."

Adair grunted as he left the room. Kaylee frowned. Behind Adair's dark magic and grumpiness, he was trying.

Ryan turned sideways on the sofa to face her.

"Tell me what's going on. Why do I feel it's much bigger than being half angel, half demon?"

After closing her eyes briefly, she told him. "You know my mother is an angel who fell from grace because she loves a demon. She was a warrior angel. And my father...he's Lucifer's eldest son."

"It makes her blood and soul a valuable commodity," Adair said as he entered the living room. He handed Kaylee a cup of hot water and a tea bag, then handed Ryan a beer. "It hasn't been opened."

Ryan took the beer and stared at Adair. Kaylee sagged against the back on the couch. After kicking off her shoes, she tucked her feet under her. She had her work cut out to get her two mates to come to terms with each other. She hoped they wouldn't make her choose. "My parents hid me in the human world to protect me from the demons. The angels don't even acknowledge my existence."

"Why is she in danger, now?" Ryan glared at Adair while he spoke the words.

Adair sat on the coffee table, putting him inches from Ryan. "Before I went to the church after you two, my brother paid me a visit. Usually Malbhor just talks shit. Random nonsense to get a rise out of me. Somehow, he knows Kaylee is my mate. Maybe it's because he's known Ryan was and assumed Kaylee was too since he took interest."

Kaylee didn't know anything about Adair's family or who Malbhor was, but she guessed he wasn't on Adair's favorite person list. She glanced at Ryan. He pressed his lips in a thin line and fisted his hands. Apparently, Ryan knew who Malbhor was and didn't like him.

Ryan met her stare and frowned. Reaching over, he cupped her cheek. "Malbhor is the bastard of all bastards. He's Lucifer's top minion."

Dread punched her in the gut. She picked up a throw pillow to her. "Is Lucifer looking for me?"

Adair shook his head. "I don't think so. If he was then I'd have heard from more than one person about you."

"We need to be sure." Ryan threaded his fingers through his hair. "Do you have a plan?"

Adair sent Ryan a crooked frown. "I thought we'd come up with one together. Tomorrow, I'll go down and see what I can find out. You two will stay here."

Ryan let out a low growl. Kaylee swung the pillow at him hitting him in the chest. "Be nice."

Ryan grabbed the pillow and tugged, bring her into his lap. "I'll be nice when he is."

She pushed off his lap and glared at both of them. "I'm going to bed. You two aren't allowed near me until you find peace with each other. Or once this thing is over, Adair removes the mark and we all go our separate ways. No mating."

Her own words burned her insides. However, she needed to make it clear to them she wouldn't put up with them being at odds.

Shaking from nervousness of ordering two alpha males around, she stomped her way down the hall to the first room she came to. The guys were going to drive her crazy until Adair told Ryan the real reason he kidnapped Tiffany.

Kaylee discovered the truth the first time she saw the demon. Although he didn't see her because she was cloaked. The angel side of her allowed her to read people—their emotions, their thoughts, their pasts. When she looked inside Adair, she found heartache and loneliness.

The demon's emotions weren't that of a regular demon. Behind the mean face he put on in front of everyone was a man who longed for what Ryan and his family had.

There had to be a reason he stole Tiffany that day. Adair believed he was doing something good.

Leaving the door to the bedroom open so she can

try to eavesdrop, she padded to the massive king size bed and crawled under the covers. Within moments, her eyes drifted shut and she as pulled into the realm of sleep.

∽

Ryan stared at the hallway where Kaylee disappeared. She just gave him and Adair an ultimatum. Did that mean she would accept both of them as mates?

Wait. Ryan hadn't accepted it. What was he thinking?

He downed the beer Adair gave him earlier. Shifters couldn't get shit-faced drunk, but Ryan wanted a comfortable numb right then. "What you did to Tiffany is unforgivable."

Adair's features softened and Ryan felt sadness and regret filter through the demon mark. It confused him. Who knew the demon had those kinds of emotions? Before he responded, Adair spoke softly. "At the time, I thought I was doing the right thing. I don't regret taking her, but I realize now how I did it was wrong. And trapping you in a bond is wrong."

"Why did you do it?" Ryan wanted to yell at him but it wouldn't do any good. They'd screamed at one other enough over the last five years. Ryan was tired of fighting.

"To save your sister's life. My brother had spotted her and watched her too closely. Usually I don't take notice of what my sick family does, but I've been watching too. Only I watched you. I knew the moment I saw you five years before, you were mine. That made Tiffany mine to protect from my brother and whatever twisted things he was plotting." Adair stood, giving Ryan his back.

Ryan stared. "Did Tiffany know?"

Adair lifted one broad shoulder in a shrug. "I told her. I don't know if she believed me. You showed up prepared to take her place as my…slave, as you put it."

There was something he wasn't saying. "If your brother was set on capturing Tiffany, then he would have gone after her once you released her."

Adair glanced over his shoulder, his gaze shone with unshed tears. "I made my own deal."

Dread slammed into Ryan. His telepathy may only work on humans, but his intuition worked just fine on all species. Adair wasn't free. "What did you do?"

Lifting the hem of his shirt, Adair turned to face Ryan. On the left side of his abs was a mark. A demon's mark. "I have to mate with you in order for your family to be free from his threat. Malbhor has been trying to collect on the debt."

Confusion mixed Ryan's thoughts up. What the hell was the demon talking about? "What debt? What. Did. You. Do?"

Adair closed his eyes and took his sweet time replying. Ryan was about to lose his patience with him before he finally spoke. "If I am unable to claim you for my mate I must return to the demon realm as his slave."

Ryan stumbled back as if someone punched him in the chest. The raw emotions coming from Adair reached out to him, wrapped around him, and squeezed. "Why would you do that?"

Adair met his gaze. Sadness clouded his dark depths. "I told you. You're mine. I mean, my mate. No one hurts my mate or his family."

Ryan understood that. It was the way of shifters. Protect the den. Protect Family. Protect their mate. Adair wasn't much different than Ryan.

Deep within, the mating urge sparked. Ryan knew it was there but the bitter anger for what Adair did blinded him from the truth. And Adair had tried to tell him over the years.

Fuck.

They had bigger issues than Ryan's pity-party. "How does he know about Kaylee?"

Adair gave a single nod. "His connection to Lucifer must be the reason he knows who her father is. But Satan doesn't want anything to do with her. It's forbidden for an angel, half breed or not, to enter Hell without consequences. That rule was created after Kaylee was born. I suspect Lucifer made the rule to keep her safe and hidden. Malbhor must have another reason."

"To use her for her power," Ryan snarled. His bear echoing his displeasure. "You have to fix this."

"I know." Adair lowered his shirt and moved passed Ryan.

Grabbing the large male by the hand, Ryan said, "Not just with Kaylee, but Tiffany too. You need to be the one to tell her the truth. Grovel. Beg her for forgiveness. Agree to be her slave for the rest of your life. Whatever it takes. If my family can't accept you, then neither can I. Mate or not."

"I know," Adair repeated.

A shimmer of light rippled in his black depths. It

was similar to when a shifter's animal looked out from within. That was the first time Ryan had ever seen it in Adair's eyes. "What type of demon are you?"

With a tilt of the head, Adair studied Ryan a moment before answering. "Half demon. My mother was a wolf shifter. My soul-stealing father killed her after I was born and took me to Hell."

∼

Adair watched the play of emotions drift across Ryan's face. Confusion, sadness, and anger were just a few of them. Squeezing Ryan's hand gently, Adair offered another piece of his tortured past. "The first time I shifted, my father beat me, then poked at the wolf. I knew instantly what he hoped to accomplish and vowed to never shift again. Because I didn't want to become a monster."

Turning away, Adair crossed the living room to the French doors leading into the sunroom. When he discovered this house, he hadn't a clue what he was doing. But it was similar to Ryan's home. Not a copy, but close in style. Adair found it comfortable and quiet.

Using his telekinesis, he willed the windows to

open. The night air filtered in. It was a mix of early spring with a bite of winter. Crisp but not cold. Adair breathed in the clean mountain breeze as he crossed to the wall of windows.

Behind him, Ryan moved closer and stopped when he stood beside Adair. After a moment of silence, Ryan asked, "Is that Blackrock?"

Adair nodded, feeling too raw, too exposed to speak.

"A demonic stalker who cares."

The tease in Ryan's tone made the corners of Adair's mouth lift. He faced Ryan. His blue eyes sparked with life and seemed to glow from within. "I can't remove the mark until I'm sure you're safe."

"You going to mark Kaylee too?" Ryan's tone was husky and sharp.

Adair blinked. He deserved all of Ryan's sarcasm and anger. "I'll spend the rest of my life making it up to you. Do you think a normal demon would allow you to live your own life?"

Ryan sighed and shook his head, then glanced out into the night. "I wondered about that."

Silence fell between them for several seconds. There was nothing else Adair could say to Ryan. It was up to the bear to forgive him. If they were truly mates as Adair believed, Ryan would have to let him in, eventually.

"My family isn't going to be so forgiving. You have a lot to make up for, especially to Tiffany. I'm not walking away from them or my pack. Blackrock is a part of me." Ryan turned to face him again. "Kaylee is my mate. I'm not walking away from her either."

"Ditto." Adair stared at the bear.

Ryan raised a brow. "Then what are we going to do?"

Adair hadn't a clue. "We need to kill my brother and make sure Kaylee's identity hasn't been revealed to everyone in Hell."

"Agreed."

"But first..." Adair closed the small space between them. "...there's something I've wanted to do since I first saw you."

He didn't give the other male a chance to reply. He dipped his head and claimed Ryan's mouth. Electrifying need shot through Adair. Raw hunger surfaced. Then he felt it. His wolf awakened for the first time in decades.

Mine. The wolf wanted Ryan and was ready to claim him on a much deeper level than the demon mark could.

When Ryan pressed his hard body into him, Adair growled and wrapped his arms around the other male. Ryan opened for him and their tongues tangled and swirled together. Hot liquid desire danced inside him.

Adair broke the kiss and rested his forehead against Ryan's. "That was..."

Ryan leaned into him. "Yeah. How long does this Stockholm syndrome last?"

Adair laughed—something he hadn't done in while. "Call it whatever you wish. You're mine."

"Yeah, yeah, stalker. We have to figure out how we're going to protect our mate." Ryan stepped out of the embrace and entered the living room, leaving Adair to watch him walk away. The male's broader shoulders and narrow waist drew his gaze to the tight ass.

Adair shook his head. *Focus. We have to plot a demon assassination.*

4

The soft dual snores coming from behind and in front of Kaylee made her smile and her heart melt. She had the urge to wake them to demand they tell her they were working out their differences—for lack of a better word. Issues didn't quiet cover it.

They were her mates. They needed to get along because if she had to choose...she'd walk away broken hearted.

Ryan stirred behind her, hugged her close, and kissed her shoulder. "Morning."

"Good morning." She rolled to her back to stare into his blue eyes. "You alright?"

He glanced at Adair, who was still sleeping, then back to her. "We will be. The mating dance is the time to work out issues and learn to trust and heal." Ryan kissed her nose. "Your safety is our priority."

She frowned. Thoughts of demons by the horde coming after her sent a shiver up her spine. Adair let out a low growl and linked his fingers with hers before bringing her hand to his lips. Instantly she relaxed.

Ryan watched Adair, but she didn't sense jealousy from him. Then Ryan sat up and stared down at her. "We have a plan."

Adair nodded and cuddled into her. Yes, he cuddled. She smiled and accepted the caring emotions from the demon by scooting closer to him. Then she felt it. A shimmer of magic similar to Ryan's shifter power.

Meeting Adair's sleepy gaze, she asked, "You're half shifter?"

"Wolf. Apparently, Ryan's bear woke my wolf up and the mutt likes to cuddle." He nuzzled her neck and threw a leg over hers. "And he likes how you smell."

"And the mixture of both your scents are driving me crazy." Ryan winked at her and shoved Adair's shoulder.

Adair moved faster than she'd ever seen anyone move. In the next moment, he had Ryan pinned to wall, his thigh between Ryan's legs. At first Kaylee froze in fear they would hurt each other. Then they kissed. She relaxed while her body heated with desire.

Mine. They were both hers. And they looked hot together.

She eased out of bed and headed to the bathroom. "You two can go over your plan with me at breakfast."

They broke apart and stared at her. With a roll of her eyes, she shut herself in the bathroom. Pressing her back against the door, she squeezed her lids shut for a brief moment. Things were happening so fast. The mating she could deal with. The unknown of how many demons knew about her unnerved her to the core.

Pushing off the door, she moved to the mirror, then pressed her palm to it. "Amriel, I need your guidance."

Her mother's image appeared instantly. Her angelic, round face brightened for a moment, then Amriel drew her brows together. "What is it dear?"

"Just wanted to ask a couple of questions."

Her mom tsked. "They must be some questions if you have to hide in a bathroom and summon me through a mirror. Really, dear. Your father and I have cell phones."

Yeah and Kaylee's phone was on the nightstand in the bedroom. She didn't want the guys knowing she called her parents. Not yet. Not until she knew exactly what she was dealing with. "Is Dad there?"

"Yes. Did you want to speak to him?"

No. "Yes." Taking a breath, Kaylee prepared herself to face her overprotective father. What she was about to tell him and ask would push his protective instincts.

Where her mother was light with golden blonde hair and pale blue eyes, her father was dark. He had black shoulder length hair and chocolate brown eyes. He stepped up behind Amriel and gave Kaylee a hard stare. "Are you in trouble?"

Kaylee opened her mouth, then shut it. She couldn't lie to parents. "Not at the moment. Maybe not at all."

Ripples of crimson flashed in his eyes a moment before he vanished. Kaylee pulled her hand from the mirror, cutting the connection. Her parents materialized behind her. With a thought, she sealed the door so the guys wouldn't hear their conversation.

Zorrol inhaled deeply and Kaylee cringed. Her father was Satan's son and just as powerful. He knew

Adair was there. Kaylee saw it in her father's pissed off, crimson glare. "You have two seconds to explain where you are and why there is a demon with you."

Involuntarily, she took a step back. Two seconds wasn't enough time to explain anything, so she gave him the short answer. "They are my mates."

Zorrol pushed passed her and exited the bathroom, breaking her spell. Kaylee's heart sank to her feet as she met her mom's apologetic gaze. Surely, he wouldn't harm her mates. Not taking the chance she turned and rushed after him. "Dad!"

She hoped the guys heard her warning. When she reached the living room, she froze. Adair faced off with her father, blocking Ryan in a protective stance while in a half-shift. His hands were claws and large fangs poked out from his upper lip.

"Adair. Why are you here?"

Dad knew him? Kaylee slowly made her way to stand beside Adair. Her father darted his gaze to her then back to her mates.

"Explain!" Her father's stern features sent a shiver through her.

She jumped at the harshness of his voice. Behind her Ryan touched her lower back and she sank into him. Adair relaxed a little and shifted back to his human form, then inched closer to her so their arms touched. She linked her fingers with his. All the while her father noted every move they made.

"Dad, this is Ryan and Adair. My mates." Kaylee straightened her spine. Although she hated fighting, she was far from weak. And she'd protect her mates at all cost.

Even from her own father if she had to.

Instead of replying to her, Zorrol addressed Adair. "It's been a long time."

Adair nodded. "A few decades at least."

Kaylee started at her father then moved her gaze to Adair. She guessed right. Her father did know him. "How do you two know each other?"

Zorrol motioned for Adair to explain. Adair scrubbed his hand over his face. "As a way to stay off my father's sadistic radar, I joined Lucifer's army. Zorrol was my commander."

Kaylee glared at her father. He never spoke of his life before he fell in love with her mom. Kaylee never asked because she simply didn't want to know about that world. Now she wish she had.

Zorrol eased his stance, like the tension fell away. "Who else knows about her?"

"My brother, Malbhor. Beyond that I'm not sure," Adair answered instantly.

Zorrol growled. "What about your father?"

"Dead. Malbhor did us that favor a few months ago."

Kaylee's mom placed a hand on Zorrol's chest, drawing his attention to her. "Go sit and we'll talk this through and plan accordingly."

After a few hesitant moments, Zorrol nodded. Kaylee relaxed and silently thanked her mom.

They all took their seats. Adair was the first to speak. "It is possible my brother only knows because he's been following me since he killed our father. I'd only found out about Kaylee's heritage two nights ago and knew instantly she was my mate. That night Malbhor showed up at my home in the Ever After, taunting me about Kaylee. I knew I had to bring her here. No one knows about this place and it is warded with protection spells."

Zorrol glanced at Kaylee. That was when she saw his fear. "I don't have to remind you that there are demons who would use her to bend Lucifer's will." He paused and released a sigh. "I'll contact my father and see if he's heard anything. He may send guards out."

Adair nodded as if he expected her father's words. "Ryan and I formed a plan to draw out Malbhor. I was going to go and see if I hear any rumors of a hybrid by throwing your name around. If it is only Malbhor running his mouth, then he dies."

Zorrol hardened his gaze on Adair. "What if there are others that know?"

Ryan answered, "Then Malbhor still dies and so does anyone who threatens her safety."

Kaylee's father stared at her mates for a long moment then nodded. "Good plan. What's the rest of it?"

The rest of it? She glanced to Adair then Ryan. They didn't look at her. Whatever it was, it was serious.

Adair cleared his throat. "We want to complete the mating but I'm not sure if doing so would also expose her to the demon realm."

Zorrol stood and began to pace. Kaylee watched her father, waiting for an explosion of anger but it never happened. After a few minutes, he stopped and faced everyone. "You will need to disconnect yourself from the demon realm. Only then can you claim her for your mate. I will not allow her to be exposed to them."

ADAIR FROWNED. Disconnect from the demon realm. His home. The only one he'd ever known. But did he consider it his home anymore? He'd never felt like he belonged. Yet he didn't belong in this realm either.

Would that change when he claimed his mates?

Meeting Zorrol's stare, Adair agreed. "Then I must start things rolling for my exit from Hell."

The other demon remained emotionless. "I'd like a word with you in private."

Adair stood and motioned to the sunroom. As they turned to leave, Kaylee protested, "Dad."

Her mother said softly, "Let them be."

Then Ryan distracted her. "We should call Tiffany so she can call off the national guard."

A soft sigh met Adair's ears. He turned and glanced at his mates. The worry in Kaylee's blue eyes tugged at his heart. He winked at her then shut the doors.

"Your father was a respected male until he caught the illness." Zorrol's word scratched against Adair's nerves.

The illness excuse was bullshit. "Dear ol' Dad was never ill. If he was, he was born with it. He just had enough control to hide his bloodlust and craving for death."

"What changed?"

Adair dropped his shoulders, then sat in an armed chair to stare off into the woods. "The death of Malbhor's mother. She was Father's true mate. My mother was a wolf shifter he stole from her own mate, marked her, impregnated her, then killed her the day I was born. I was the reminder of my mother's rejection."

Zorrol dropped in a chair across from Adair. "I thought walking away from my family and Hell would be hard. It wasn't. Amriel and Kaylee is my family. They are my life."

Adair let out a humorless chuckle. "I've walked away long before I met Ryan. At least I tell myself that when in reality my brother holds me there."

"Why do you think so?"

"Because I fucking care too much. For Ryan and his family. Now for Kaylee. I don't understand the feelings, but I know I'd kill to protect them." Adair waved a hand and the windows opened. The scent of rain drifted in.

Zorrol conjured a couple of cigars and handed one to him. "I didn't want to say anything in front of Kaylee or her mother, but I'm still in contact with Lucifer. He runs recon throughout Hell to make sure any rumors about me, Amriel, and Kaylee end before they get started. If your brother is still alive, then he hasn't said anything."

Adair stared at Zorrol, then raised a brow as the meaning behind his words sank in. "So you keep the earthside demons in line for Satan?"

A half smile formed on the demon's mouth. "Someone has to."

"You think your mate is clueless?"

Zorrol laughed. "She knows. She just pretends she doesn't. But Kaylee doesn't."

Good. "She won't learn it from me."

A long, comfortable silence fell over them as they smoked their cigars. During that time Adair thought about when his brother taunted him about Kaylee. He wasn't sure Malbhor actually knew Kaylee was Zorrol's daughter. That might had been why Adair thought his brother was lying.

"We focus on Malbhor, then. But promise me something."

Zorrol nodded. "What?"

"I make the death blow."

"Done."

5

Ryan handed Kaylee his phone. "You call her."

Kaylee laughed but took the phone. "Chicken."

"No, I'm a bear, remember?" He loved bringing a smile to her face after she was so anxious about her dad and Adair disappearing into the sunroom to talk. "Besides, the tension is gone from Adair. He's actually determined and a little more focused."

"That's good." Kaylee dialed Tiffany's number and put it on speaker. "Tif knows my mom is an angel."

But not about her dad. Ryan knew that. Kaylee had told him she hadn't told her she was part demon.

Tiffany answered on the first ring. "Where the hell are you?"

Kaylee smiled. "Hello, Tiffany."

"Kaylee! Oh, thank the gods. Where are you? Wait. Where is Ryan?"

Hearing his sister's voice relaxed his bear. He hadn't realized how much he missed his family, even though it'd only been a little more than twenty-four hours. "Right here, baby sis."

"Ryan." His name came out as a whispered sob. It broke his heart to hear her cry. He should have called her last night.

"Hey, I'm alright. Kaylee is safe. We'll will be home soon."

Kaylee took his hand in hers and squeezed. "Tiffany, I'm sorry but I won't be at work tomorrow. I might need to take the rest of the week off."

"A week! Ryan?"

Rustling sounded then a click sounded before Holt's, Tiffany's mate, voice came over the connection. "Just tell us what we can do."

We? "Is the whole family there?" Ryan glanced at Amriel who pressed her lips together to keep from laughing.

Anthony, his oldest brother, said, "You bet your ass. Give us the status and plan."

Ryan sighed. He wasn't ready for a family meeting. "Kaylee and I are with Adair." There, he ripped that bandage off. He wasn't adding to it by announcing the demon was his mate. That info would have to wait until later. "He has a house just outside of pack land. No, I'm not telling you where. It's secure and we're okay."

"Why would it need to be secure while you are with the demon?" The growled out question came from his father, Elijah Black.

Ryan let out a growl of his own. "Things are complicated. We have bigger issues that Adair and I are handling. I can't come home right now because it would put the den in danger. You will have to trust me for now."

There was a long silence. Kaylee put his phone on mute and said, "Just tell them if it will help."

Ryan shook his head. "My father would send the enforcers out to help us. There are too many unknowns right now to put them in danger. Plus, the alpha's youngest son is just as protected as the Heir. I'll keep them on a need to know basis. It's better."

He cupped Kaylee's cheek then leaned in to place a kiss on her lips. "The fewer of us there are, the better it would be to track Malbhor"

Kaylee leaned into him and nodded. "I guess."

"Ryan! Take us off mute."

He laughed at Tiffany's tone. The baby of the

family was so protective of everyone. He pressed the mute button. "Adair needs our help with something."

"I'm sure the demon has an alternative motive. What if he's working with his brother to set a trap for you?" Tiffany's voice started to shake.

Ryan's chest tightened. He hated lying to his family. Then the phone clicked again and his father's voice came over the line. "Do what you need to. Take the time you need. Tiffany will be okay. If you need anything, call or send us a signal of some kind."

Relaxing, Ryan nodded. "Thanks, Dad. We'll be in touch."

The call ended and he stared at Kaylee. She smiled and showed him her phone. "I texted your mom. I know we said we'd keep it to ourselves, but I think the Alpha needs to know what's up. He can prepare…just in case."

Relief flooded him. He read the messages and chuckled. She was right. His parents did need to know. Wrapping an arm around Kaylee, he hugged her close. "Thanks."

The messages gave his parents the short version of the facts he didn't want Tiffany knowing right now. That Kaylee was Satan's granddaughter and Adair was their mate. His mom was great at reading between the lines and connecting the dots, so he trusted her to settle things at home so he could deal with his mates.

The French doors to the sunroom opened and Adair met his gaze. "What happened?"

Ryan shook his head. "Just called home."

Amriel stood and drifted to her mate, wrapping her arms around his waist. "We are here if you need us."

The three of them nodded as the couple dematerialized.

Adair added, "Do you need to go home?"

"No." Ryan studied him. That was a first for the demon to offer to let Ryan go home. Was he truly changing?

Yes. As much as Ryan fought it over the last few years, he saw the changes in the demon. He just needed to stop and listen to the truth.

Holding out a hand, he said, "Come here."

Adair moved closer. When he took Ryan's hand, Ryan pulled him down onto the couch. The demon landed on his back, laying across Ryan's and Kaylee's lap. The connection of the three of them, so close, made Ryan's bear groan. "What's the plan?"

"The same. Zorrol says Lucifer has a tighter control on the rumor mill. If someone mentions Kaylee's name or her parents, it's shut down immediately." Adair glanced up at Kaylee, then reach up to caress her cheek.

She closed her eyes. Ryan hardened. Damn his mates were hot. Shaking out of his desire filled thoughts, he said, "So we draw out Malbhor."

"Yep. I want to give him a day or so before I summon him." A wicked smile formed on Adair's lips.

"You can summon him?"

Adair nodded. "Just like she can summon her parents."

Kaylee laughed. "I called them to find out info. I didn't think my father would actually show up."

"Um huh." Adair pushed to a stand, then took Kaylee's hand, tugging her to a stand. "I think we need to take our mate to bed."

Ryan was so on board with that. "Yeah. She's been sneaking around. She deserves to be teased until she begs us to stop."

"You two are wicked. I may have to reconsider this mating thing." Kaylee let out a squeal when Adair scooped her up in his arms and carried her to the bedroom.

6

Kaylee squealed as Adair dropped her in the middle of his bed, then nibbled her bottom lip as he stared down at her. Streaks of crimson swirled in his dark chocolate, desire-filled gaze. Her body heated like a wildfire consuming her.

Movement behind the demon catch her attention. Ryan prowled around to the other side of the bed, while locking gazes with her. Anticipations made her pussy ache and pulse with need. Her nipples hardened, and each movement made them scrape against her bra. Tingles of pleasure skittered over her skin while pulses of pleasure arched off each nerve.

Damn, she was on fire and they hadn't touched her yet.

On the heels of that thought, both guys crawled on

the bed. Ryan was the first to slide his hand across her belly over the night gown she still wore. She inhaled, trying to calm her hammering heart as he slid that hand down her abs and farther. When he cupped her over her panties, she bucked, lifting her bottom off the bed.

Holly hell. Her panties were soaked. Pleasure rolled through her, increasing the achy desire consuming her. "Skin. I need—"

A low rumble, almost a growl came from Adair. She glanced at him and they locked gazes. Her heart hammered, and her breaths increased in anticipation. He dipped his head and claimed her mouth, thrusting his tongue inside.

Instantly, she reached for him, cupping him through his jeans.

There was no denying they were her mates. Every part of her screamed it. She'd had sex a few times and nothing compared to the raw hunger these two males ignited within her.

Ryan's hand grazed her thigh and she sucked in a breath, breaking the kiss with Adair. A low chuckle escaped Ryan before he said, "So wet...and beautiful."

He yanked her gown up and ripped her panties from her. Oh yes. The bear knew what she needed.

She spread her thighs, giving him a better view. Ryan growled, then lowered his head to place a kiss on her clit. His tongue came out, slid through her folds, and teased the bundle of nerves.

Her body jerked, then she moved against his face.

Adair hardened even more under her hand. With a growl of his own, he pushed her hand away and moved off the bed. He returned to her a moment later, his pants removed and cock freed for her to admire. He kissed the other side of her neck, biting and sucking.

Pleasure rolled through her over and over. She didn't know how much longer she was going to last before she started begging.

Adair nipped at her skin as he made his way down her collarbone to her breast. He captured a nipple in his mouth. Gripping him in her hand, she slowly stroked. A hiss of a groan escaped Adair, and he moved his hips in time with her strokes.

He cupped one of her breasts, rolling the nipple between his fingers. Pinpricks of pleasure crawled over her skin. Pulsing need grew, almost becoming too much.

Ryan only added to her mounting pleasure with

his licks. Then he stopped and lifted his head to watch them. "I want to watch you suck him."

Focusing on Adair's hard cock, she smiled and guided it to her mouth. She licked the tip, teasing and drawing a moan from him.

"It's not nice to tease." Adair growled and fisted a hand in her hair.

She took him into her mouth at the same time Ryan slid two fingers inside her and rubbed her clit with his thumb. Good God, she'd never felt like she did in that moment. Desired. Sexy. And...wild.

While she sucked Adair, she heard the zipper of Ryan's pants, and she whimpered. Want turned into raw, hot desire. The thought of having her bear shifter buried deep inside her almost made her come.

When Ryan guided his cock into her, she released Adair on a gasp as pleasure washed over her, drowning her with desire.

Adair moved so he could take a nipple into his mouth and began stroking his cock.

So many sensations. She didn't know whether to hold on and let it keep building or just succumb to the pleasure and dive over the edge.

Ryan seemed to be making the decision for her— or making it harder to hold onto the control—he increased his thrusts, pounding into her. The moment she cried out in release, both her males did, too.

Ryan eased down to lay half on top of her, his cock buried deep inside like he didn't want to lose the connection.

Adair reached up and cupped her face. He laughed and said, "The two of you are beautiful."

He heart melted more. In that moment, she wanted nothing more than to be with both of them. As their mate.

To hell with the dangers that lay ahead of them.

7

It'd been two days since the three of them formed a plan to summon and kill Malbhor. Only Malbhor wasn't answering the call.

Adair was about to tear through Hell to search for his brother.

Pacing the small living room of his home in the Ever After, Adair went over the possibilities of where the asshat would be hiding. Nothing came to mind. Malbhor just showed up when he wasn't wanted.

He tried one more time before returning to his mates. Closing his eyes, he focused on his brother's essence. "Malbhor. I summon you."

A few seconds later, the bastard materialized in front of him. "You rang?"

"Your time is up. You lied to me about Kaylee. It is true she is half demon, but she is no relation to

Lucifer. Her mother is human." Adair put all his power into his words to make his brother believe them.

Malbhor shrugged. "Can't be right all the time."

The tone he used didn't sit right with Adair. It was too uncaring. Like his brother wasn't after Kaylee at all. Then what did he want? "What do you want?"

"For you to suffer." Malbhor started to circle him. "You see...you were the reason my mother was unhappy. You drove her to end her own life. The constant reminder of the whore Father was unfaithful with."

No. Not possible. "Your mother was Father's true mate. He wouldn't be able to bed another."

Malbhor tsked as he shook his head slowly. "You live in a fairytale of mates. It's shifters who mate for life. Demons can fuck who they want when they want."

Adair stepped back. Was that true? Had his father, when he was alive, truly been ill with bloodlust?

Shaking off his brother's words, Adair faced his brother a little straighter. "You're lying. Your mother was just as evil as you and Father."

And he was stalling.

Adair raised his hand and formed a fireball and thrust it toward his brother. "You will never harm me or mine ever again."

"You're wrong. I already have." Those were Malbhor's last words before the fire consumed him, turning him to black ash on the floor.

A sudden wave of fear followed by anger, then pain washed over him. Then a vision formed. Ryan and Kaylee were under attack.

Demons stormed the home Adair believed was secure.

No! Adair teleported back to his earthside home.

Everything was as he left it. Clean. "Ryan. Kaylee."

"In here." Ryan called from the sunroom.

Adair exited and breathed a sigh of relief. Kaylee stepped toward him. "What is it?"

He hugged her tight, while holding out an arm for Ryan. The bear came to him instantly. The three of them embraced. "Malbhor is dead. Then I had a vision that you were attacked."

"We are safe." Kaylee said. "Dad and I strengthened the wards this morning after you left. Your brother wanted to torment you one last time."

Breathing in deep, he realized she was right. The

magic surrounding the house was stronger than he'd ever felt it. No demon could penetrate the wards. His mates were safe.

"I need to feel both of you...inside and out."

Ryan claimed his lips, thrusting his tongue inside his mouth. Adair groaned and hardened. When Ryan broke the kiss, he said, "I accept you and Kaylee as my mates."

Adair's heart filled with love. He knew that's what it had to be because he'd never felt so complete and fulfilled all at once.

He glanced at Kaylee and she gave both them a shy smile. "I accept both you as my mates, but you have to catch me first."

She darted through the living room and toward the bedroom. Adair and Ryan laughed and chased their mate.

∼

Kaylee braced herself for impact. She barely had time to remove her clothes before her mates entered the room, desire in their gazes.

Her flesh heated as they prowled closer to her.

Then her panties dampened. Good God, she was going to die from pleasure. At least she'd go happy.

"Wait." She held up a hand. "I'm not being hunted anymore, right?"

"Only by us." Ryan smirked.

A slow smile lifted her lips. "Good. Then, I claim and accept both of you as my mates."

She kissed Ryan as Adair moved to stand behind her. Magical threads of crimson, white, and black swirled around them, wrapping them in a bond, then fusing to their souls. Her heart beat in time with her mates. Their emotions and thoughts were hers to feel and see.

Linking her fingers with Adair's and then Ryan's, she held onto the connection, never wanting to let go of them.

But her bliss was chased away by a summon from her father. The guys felt it too and stared at her. With a sigh, she stepped out of their embrace, willed her clothes back on, and called out to her parents. "You may enter."

Her parents materialized in front of her. Kaylee crossed her arms, "I do have a cell phone."

Her father frowned then scanned the room as if searching for something. "Ryan, check in with your father."

Ryan didn't ask questions, just pulled out his cell and punched father's number, then put it on speaker.

Elijah answered on the first ring. "Ryan, you've been recruited to head up the bear sentinels."

Ryan's face paled. Kaylee heard Tiffany talk about the sentinels. It was a new group of shifter enforcers where packs and clans in the area banded together in fighting rogues. They'd hoped to control the rogue population before another pack war, like the one Ashwood Falls won a few months ago.

The bears had wanted to stay neutral. Kaylee guessed something had happened to force their hand.

"What happened?" Ryan tone carried the alpha power he got from his father.

"There's been reports coming in from all over the southeast of demon attacks. Right now, it seems wolf packs are the most affected." Elijah paused and Kaylee glanced at Adair, who had also paled. "Ryan, I need you to come home. Bring your mates. Adair could be of aid as well."

The call ended.

Everyone in the room was silent for several minutes. Finally, Adair, whispered. "This is my fault. Before I killed Malbhor, he said he wanted me to suffer." His eyes widened as if realizing something.

"The attacks on the wolf dens are a distraction. He said it was done. Made me believe it was you two. He made Blackrock a target."

8

By the time they reached Blackrock demons were already on the attack. A couple of buildings and homes were on fire while others had holes in them like a car had crashed into them. Debris littered the streets. Cars were overturned. Furniture and appliances scattered through the lawns. Trees were uprooted.

It was a war zone.

Ryan fisted his hands and a fierce roar ripped from him. On his right, Adair echoed his roar then the male shifted into a beautiful black wolf. When he glanced at Ryan, his eyes were red, showing his demon side.

On Ryan's left, Kaylee let out a growl. Her hands began to glow in a blue fire. Was that angel fire? Then she charged forward into the den. With a curse, Ryan ran after her while Adair took off to his right.

"Ryan!"

Tiffany's scream sliced through his heart. He stopped and glanced her way. His blood ran cold at the sight of a large demon with purple-ish skin and huge horns sticking out of his forehead lifting her in the air.

Kaylee rushed to his side and let out growl that made his bear proud. "Fucking demons. There's too many of them."

"Go find Adair and see if there is something the three of us can do."

Kaylee grabbed his arm. "What are you going to do?"

Meeting her glare, he gave her a crooked grin, then kissed her. "I'm going to get my sister."

He didn't wait for Kaylee to argue. He took off in a run then leaped in the air and shifted into his large, black bear. His claw made contact with the demon's face and Ryan jerked downward, leaving four gashes in the bastard's face. The impact of Ryan's claws hitting the demon knocked him off balance. He released Tiffany and she screamed as she fell to the ground, shifting just before she landed. Pissed, Ryan leaped at the demon again and hit him in the head.

The male stumbled and fell on his ass. But Ryan didn't let up. No one hurt his sister or anyone in his clan.

A magical charge zapped through the air a moment before Kaylee's dad materialized beside Ryan. Zorrol curled his lip and thrust a hand out, toward the other demon. "Return to Hell."

As soon as the last word left Zorrol's lips the demon vanished. Ryan stared at Zorrol. His new father-in-law shook his head. "No time to explain."

Right. *"Kaylee is with Adair."* Ryan sent the telepathic thought to him. Wherever the hell that was.

Zorrol nodded and dematerialized. Apparently, he knew where his daughter was.

Ryan turned to Tiffany, his heart stopping for a long moment. She was so still. No, no, no. *Tiff, get up.* He nudged her face with his nose. She blinked open her eyes and Ryan sagged in relief. Shifting back to human, he conjured a pair of jeans on—thanks to the power he gained from being marked and bonded to Adair. He gathered his baby sister in his arms. Well as much as he could. She was twice his size in her bear form.

The pounding of footsteps made Ryan snap his head up. He growled, then relaxed. Anthony and Holt—Tiff's mate—stopped next to them. Holt knelt down and pulled Tiffany from Ryan. "Are you okay?"

Ryan didn't reply because he knew the male was talking to Tiffany. She shifted back to human and Ryan gave his attention to Anthony, giving the couple privacy even though they all grew up together and nakedness was a common occurrence among shifters. "What's up?"

"There's too many of them." Anthony threaded a hand through his hair.

"Zorrol just got here. He's like Lucifer's son."

A growl ripped from Anthony, his alpha power from being the Heir and Marshal of Blackrock slammed into Ryan. He stepped back but glared at his brother. Anthony spoke first. "You brought the demon general here? Are you fucking out of your mind?"

Ryan straightened and shoved his brother. "Zorrol is on our side. He's Kaylee's father."

Behind him Tiffany gasped. Ryan closed his eyes briefly. "Look, now is not the time to explain any of this."

A boom sounded and the ground shook. Then pain ignited in Ryan's chest. "Kaylee."

He ran to the center of the den, his brothers and sister following close behind him. When they reached the circle they held rituals and ceremonies in, they skidded to a stop. In the center of the circle was Kaylee, her parents, and Ryan's father. They stood with their backs to each other. Magic, dark and white, swirled around them. And they were chanting.

Adair spotted him from the other side and made his way to him. Anthony growled as Adair stepped up next to Ryan. Placing a hand on his brother's chest, Ryan met his stare. "Like it or not, Adair is my mate." Turning to Adair, Ryan pointed to the circle. "What's going on?"

"They are sending the demons back to where they belong and securing the den." Adair reached for him and Ryan took his hand and leaned into him.

"What was that boom?"

"Our demonic angel. You should have seen her. She lured the demons to the circle and showed them what happens when you mess with what belongs to her." Adair laughed. "I've never seen anything like it. She sent out a magical blast that wiped out the bastards. Those who lived through it ran back to Hell with their tails between their legs."

An hour later, Ryan stood with his arm folded, listening to his siblings argue over having a demon live in the den. At first Ryan figured they'd just agree to disagree and give Adair a second chance. That wasn't going to happen.

Tapping Adair on the shoulder and taking Kaylee by the hand, he led them out of the den. He'd had enough. If his family wasn't going to accept his mates, then he'd leave.

His nose tingled at the decision, but he couldn't live one place while his mates were someplace else.

Kaylee wrapped an arm around his waist. "Everything will work out."

She was right. His family was close and no matter what happened, they love him. And they'd have to love his mates too. Some day.

Kaylee let go of him and ran ahead. "I'll race you home and I'll be naked. Don't make me wait."

She dematerialized.

Ryan and Adair cursed at the same and teleported home. To their mate.

They took form in the bedroom. Their demonic angel was naked and laid across the massive bed. Ryan stripped down, but Adair beat him to it by using his magic to remove his clothes.

Instead of joining them right away, Ryan

admired their naked forms wrapped around one another. So, beautiful. And all his.

"Have I told you two how much I love you?"

Kaylee laughed and threw a pillow at him. "You don't have to. We feel it in the mating bond. Now get over here. I need both of you inside me now."

"Yes ma'am." Ryan crawled on bed and trailed kisses up her leg to the inside of her thigh. Then he nipped at the sensitive skin.

She groaned and fisted her hand in his hair. "No teasing."

Ignoring her, he licked her clit then covered her with his mouth. She bucked under him and start moaning. Glancing up, he watched Adair took one of her nipples between his teeth. Fuck. He was going to come before he was ready.

Sitting up on his knees, he gripped her hips and thrust inside her. She cried in pleasure. Desire heated his insides. Love and passion flooded the bonding link between them.

Adair moved up the bed and Kaylee took him into her mouth. His mates were trying to kill him. *So fucking hot.*

In that moment, they were one. Pleasure bounced between with each thrust in and out. Kaylee milked, then tightened around his cock right before she screamed out as the she came. Ryan and Adair followed with an orgasm of their own.

Panting and breathless, Ryan snuggled up between his mates. "I love you. Both of you."

"We love you too."

Just then his phone rang. Frowning, he glanced at his mates. Adair handed him the cell. "Hello."

"You left." Tiffany's tone sounded sad.

"You all were arguing. I'm not listening to it. How would you feel if it was Holt who was the outcast? You couldn't live without him." Ryan closed his eyes. The rock on his chest was back.

"We're not making you choose." She fell silent. After a few moments she added, "Kaylee's part demon and she's good."

"Adair is only half demon."

"I know. Dad told me. He also said Kaylee's father showed him the truth. That Adair was protecting me the only way he knew how." She sighed. "Come to dinner tomorrow night. Bring your mates. I can't lose my brother."

Tears blurred Ryan's eyes. Too many emotions for one day. He chuckled and teased his sister. "You have two other brothers."

"You're not funny right now." She still laughed.

"If you trust him enough to mate him, then I'll try too."

That was all he needed to hear. "I love you, Tiff. See you tomorrow."

"Love you too, Ry." She hung up.

Kaylee kissed his cheek. "I told you everything would work out."

Yeah, she did. The light in their darkness. He kissed her hard, then tickled her. "Don't be a smarty pants."

"I have to be the smart one." She jumped up and ran to the bathroom.

Ryan and Adair shared a wicked look before chasing their mate.

Who knew that one demon mark would lead him to a triad and a lifetime of pleasure and love.

The End

NOTE FROM LIA

Hello Readers!

Ryan's story is a long time coming. I'm happy to finally get his story out and share it with you all.

Many of you may ask is this it for Blackrock? My answer is no, not really. I have one more planned that will crossover with the Shifter of Ashwood Falls series and merge with the new series arc. I'm just not sure on where it all fits together.

With that said, look for new Ashwood Falls books to come in 2019. We will start a read a long with the series in my fan club group. So come join in the fun. Join the fan club here: https://www.facebook.com/groups/LiaDavisFanClub/

Happy Reading!

Lia

ABOUT THE AUTHOR

In 2008, Lia Davis ventured into the world of writing and publishing and never looked back. She has published more than twenty books, including the bestselling *A Tiger's Claim*, book one in her fan favorite Ashwood Falls series. Her novels feature compassionate yet strong alpha heroes who know how to please their women and her leading ladies are each strong in their own way. No matter what obstacle she throws at them, they come out better in the end.

While writing was initially a way escape from real world drama, Lia now makes her living creating worlds filled with magic, mystery, romance, and adventure so that *others* can leave real life behind for a few hours at a time.

Lia's favorite things are spending time with family, traveling, reading, writing, chocolate, coffee, nature and hanging out with her kitties. She and her family live in Northeast Florida battling hurricanes and very humid summers, but it's her home and she loves it! Sign up for her newsletter, become a member of her fan club, and follow her on Twitter @NovelsByLia.

Follow Lia on Social Media
Website: http://www.authorliadavis.com/
Newsletter: http://www.subscribepage.com/authorliadavis.newsletter
Facebook author fan page: https://www.facebook.com/novelsbylia/
Facebook Fan Club: https://www.facebook.com/groups/LiaDavisFanClub/
Twitter: https://twitter.com/novelsbylia
Tumblr: http://novelsbylia.tumblr.com/

ALSO BY LIA DAVIS

Paranormals

Ashwood Falls Series

Winter Eve

A Tiger's Claim

A Mating Dance

Surrendering to the Alpha

A Rebel's Heart

Divided Loyalties

Touch of Desire

A Leopard's Path

Jaguar's Judgment

Bears of Blackrock

Bear Essentials

Bear Magick

A Beary Sweet Holiday

Bear Marked

Dragons of Ares

War's Passion

Ashes of War

Artemis's Hunt

Chaotic War

Sons of War Box Set: Volume One

Shifting Magick Trilogy

Moon Curse

Moon Kissed

Moon Mated

Shifting Magick Trilogy box set

The Divinities

Forgotten Visions

Death's Storm

Singles Titles

First Contact

Ghost in the Bottle (co-written with Kerry Adrienne)

Contemporaries

Pleasures of the Heart Series

Business Pleasures

Single Titles

His Guarded Heart

NOTE FROM THE PUBLISHER

Thank you for reading the **Bears of Blackrock.** If you liked the stories, please leave a review. Reviews help the authors more than you know.

If you'd like to know more about After Glows, check out our website or email us at admin@AfterGlowsPublishing.com.

To stay current with upcoming titles, new releases, and other publishing news from After Glows subscribe to our MAILING LIST.

Also, join our Facebook Reader's Group to interact with our authors and other readers.

Thank you again for purchasing and reading **Bears of Blackrock.**.

Made in the USA
Coppell, TX
23 October 2019